"Stop."

"Why?"

"You don't know what you're doing. What you're asking for," Matthieu stated, almost angrily.

"I may be naive—"

"May be? You are an innocent, Maria. A true innocent."

"Does that mean I don't know what I want?"

"It means you don't understand the implications of what you want."

"Would anyone?" she asked.

"This is something that you should do with someone capable of staying with you."

No one ever stays, her mind voiced, batting away each and every one of his arguments. She knew, deep down, that this was what she wanted with her entire being. She had never been more sure of anything, half-fearful that if he walked away now she would have lost something that she had only dreamed of in the darkest of nights and the deepest of sleeps.

"I haven't asked for anything more than this night."

Pippa Roscoe lives in Norfolk near her family and makes daily promises to herself that *this* is the day she'll leave the computer to take a long walk in the countryside. She can't remember a time when she wasn't dreaming about handsome heroes and innocent heroines. Totally her mother's fault, of course—she gave Pippa her first romance to read at the age of seven! She is inconceivably happy that she gets to share those daydreams with you all. Follow her on Twitter, @pipparoscoe.

Books by Pippa Roscoe

Harlequin Presents

Conquering His Virgin Queen
Virgin Princess's Marriage Debt

The Winners' Circle

A Ring to Take His Revenge
Claimed for the Greek's Child
Reclaimed by the Powerful Sheikh

Visit the Author Profile page
at Harlequin.com for more titles.

Pippa Roscoe

——

DEMANDING HIS
BILLION-DOLLAR HEIR

Recycling programs for this product may not exist in your area.

ISBN-13: 978-1-335-14837-7

Demanding His Billion-Dollar Heir

Copyright © 2020 by Pippa Roscoe

This edition published by arrangement with Harlequin Books S.A.

For questions and comments about the quality of this book, please contact us at CustomerService@Harlequin.com.

Harlequin Enterprises ULC
22 Adelaide St. West, 40th Floor
Toronto, Ontario M5H 4E3, Canada
www.Harlequin.com

Printed in U.S.A.

DEMANDING HIS
BILLION-DOLLAR HEIR

For Jasmine Rowlandson, whose incredible jewelry and sculptures ignited a wonderful spark of inspiration that became Maria.

CHAPTER ONE

STUPID, STUPID, STUPID.

What on earth had she done? Maria had fled the opulent ballroom of the Hotel La Sereine after her argument with Theo—shaking and shivering at the devastation she'd seen in both his and his fiancée's eyes, the moment she'd accidentally revealed Theo's plans to leave Sofia at the altar. Theo Tersi—the man she thought she'd loved for nearly six years.

But, she hadn't. She'd realised it the moment she'd seen the horror and grief on the faces of the engaged couple. Nothing she'd ever felt for Theo had engendered that much…pain. Maria Rohan de Luen sucked in a huge lungful of air around the tears that were now freefalling from her cheeks. Tears for them, for herself. Because she *knew* that she'd destroyed something between them that she'd been looking for herself for so, so long. Knew that what she'd *thought* she'd felt for Theo was nothing more than the desperate need to… be loved?

She cursed herself for that weakness. Part of her

desperately wanted to go back, to find Sofia and explain, to apologise to Theo...but truly she feared she'd do more harm than good and instead, after taking one step forward and one back, collapsed onto the soft grass banking the smooth, mirror-like surface of the lake stretching out beneath the night sky.

She resisted the urge to peek into the depths of the water, reluctant to see what would be reflected back at her. Her hand grasped the cool glass neck of the bottle of champagne she'd been blindly holding as she'd hurled words that threatened to sever the bond between two people who very clearly loved each other. She'd never much had a taste for the stuff, but if there was ever a time to get blind drunk, at twenty-two years old, Maria decided that surely now was it.

Part of her was conscious that she was on the verge of over-indulging in self-pity, and the other part wanted to punish, believing that she didn't even deserve that selfish act. Not after what she'd just done.

Theo, her older brother's best friend, had loomed-large in her life, ever since her sixteenth birthday. Sebastian and Theo had become almost instantly joined at the hip after a mutually beneficial business deal and there wasn't a family memory in the last six years that didn't have them both in it. Maria bit back a laugh at her inner thought's use of the word 'family'. She hadn't seen her father or stepmother in almost eighteen months. And she was fine with that. In some ways they factored so little in her day to day life that occasionally a random thought or memory would catch her by surprise and remind her of them.

She wondered what her father would think of her and what had just happened. He'd probably give her that gaze, the one that said he wasn't really seeing *her*, but another woman—one he had loved so all-consumingly that he'd not been able to recover from the loss of her. Then he'd almost start when Maria would speak because it only served to show that she wasn't her mother, no matter how similar they might have looked.

She had nothing else of her mother, no memories, no heirlooms—Valeria, her stepmother, had seen to that— save but one necklace. The one she wore, *always*, even though it served as both an anchor and a homage to a woman who had died giving her life.

So no, while exiled Duke Eduardo Rohan de Luen would have been as ineffectual as always on the subject of what had just happened, Valeria would have sniffed in contempt and been only gleeful whilst declaring that she'd always known *'that boy'*, Theo Tersi, would cause nothing but trouble.

And Theo's crime? Guilt by association. Valeria had never forgiven Sebastian for the drastic measures he'd had to take to save their family from complete and utter destruction. When Maria had been eight, Eduardo had doubled down on an incredibly risky oil investment in the Middle East and lost not only his own money, but a large portion belonging to other members of Spain's nobility. A shocking and shameful moment that had seen the Rohan de Luens exiled from Spain, yet allowed to keep their hereditary title.

The only thing that had kept them from bankruptcy had been Seb who, at eighteen, had taken control of the financial purse strings and done what was needed. This included selling off almost every single piece of property and valuable item that wasn't nailed down. And for a woman who had only married Eduardo for prestige and money, Valeria hadn't taken it well at all.

For Maria? It had meant leaving behind everything she'd ever known, moving to Italy from Spain, and starting all over again. But in her heart, she'd known that the damage was already done. Suddenly unsure about even the most seemingly permanent things in life, Maria had withdrawn from friends and education, choosing instead to lose herself in her art and sculpture.

Until London's Camberwell College of Arts had accepted her on a foundation course, and she'd fallen utterly in love with the place, the people and the freedom she'd found away from her family. The friends she'd made during her degree, the little flat-share she lived in... Now, sitting on the bank of the river, all she wanted was to be back there.

She groaned out loud into the night sky and pressed the heels of her palms into the orbs of her eyes.

Oh, God, what had she done?

'Is this seat taken?'

From the first moment Matthieu had seen the figure down by Lac Peridot, some strange sense of self-preservation told him to walk away. *Run.* From the empty veranda sweeping around the ballroom of the Iondorran hotel where a charity gala was being held, he'd seen the white lace dress worn by the dark-haired woman glowing in the moonlight. Tendrils of her long, gently curled hair had hung almost down to her hips and the sudden memory of his mother's favourite painting stole his breath. He'd not seen or thought of the painting for years and when the figure had turned, for just a moment, back to the ballroom, something in her features, as clearly picked out by the moonbeams as her dress, had called to him as if across the years.

Matthieu Montcour knew better than to approach a woman so clearly lost in her own private thoughts, but he couldn't help himself. There was something almost tragically beautiful about her. And Matthieu had had his fair share of tragedy. He knew how life could be one thing in one moment and an entirely new thing in another.

He'd been about to turn away from the figure and the direction of thoughts he rarely visited, when he saw her inexpertly take a swig from the champagne bottle, failing to account for the back flow of the bubbles, and nearly smiled as the froth rushed from the mouth of the bottle forcing the woman to lean out of the way as the alcohol funnelled onto the grass beside her. Nearly smiled, because smiling was something Matthieu did very little of. The figure gave up, indelicately wiping her mouth with the back of her wrist, placing the bottle in the nest of skirts she'd made between her legs and went back to studying the lake. The carelessness about her clothing spoke to her distraction. This was no skilled seductress, his usual preferred companion. There was an innocence about her, shining, glowing, and all the more reason for him to stay away. But something about her drew him in—even though he was the last person to play white knight. No. He was the beast that mothers warned their daughters about.

Yet for the first time in years, he simply couldn't deny himself the urge to take a closer look at the woman who had caught his eye and imagination. He'd stepped away from the veranda, leaving the sights and sounds of the ballroom behind him, and slowly padded his way over the soft grass, pulling up about a metre away from where she sat.

'Is this seat taken?'

She started, peering up at him from her seat on the grass, momentary shock painting her features that righted themselves back to neutral. He'd chosen English—it being the most widely used at the gala and, as such, he figured it a safe bet, given that it was highly unlikely she spoke Swiss French.

'Standing room only, I'm afraid.'

Her response surprised him, as much as her gentle European accent. Spanish perhaps? Maybe Italian? Taking his shock for persistence, she finally inclined her head.

'Pull up a pew,' she invited.

Frowning again, and confused instantly—which was untenable to Matthieu—he chose to comment. 'That's a very English turn of phrase for such a European accent.'

'That's a very round about way of asking me where I'm from.'

And whilst Matthieu decidedly didn't like confusion, he found the slightly circuitous bent of her conversation appealing. Too many women, once they knew who he was, decided upon a brute-force attack of the sensual kind, the only thing that he would respond to. But he didn't see that jolt of recognition in her eyes. When she'd finally turned to take him in, the woman seemed only to pass over his features as if gazing over a far horizon. And damn him if there wasn't a part of him that was pleased by that.

He took a seat beside her on the comfortable grass and felt a sigh of relief escape him. He was glad to be away from the ballroom. He hated this part of his role as CEO for Montcour Mining Industries. 'Schmoozing', Malcolm called it. Matthieu preferred to call it a waste of time. But he knew better than to argue with his Managing Director, oldest friend, and one-time legal guardian. The Iondorran Minister for Trade had decided that the charity gala would be a neutral arena to test the waters of a possible joint mining venture within the small European country. Matthieu was slightly on the fence about it—unsure as to whether Iondorra actually had the financial infrastructure to take on such an ambitious project. But he wasn't ready to shoot it out of the water completely. Not yet anyway. These days

Matthieu was incredibly choosy about his ventures, simply because he could be.

He saw, from the corner of his eye, the woman beside him—young, he noticed now that he was closer—wipe discreetly at her cheek. A blade of grass, or a bubble of champagne from earlier? A tear perhaps?

The action had released a trail of perfume, wafting towards him on the warm night air, teasing his senses with tones of woody sage and something almost like the sea…salt, he realised. Inexplicably his mouth watered, desire creeping through his body.

'Would you like some?'

He shook his head at the bottle she nudged with her knee. Matthieu rarely drank, refusing to allow anything to dull his senses to such an extent. But in the back of his mind, he wondered if he was already part drunk on the woman and the situation he found himself in.

They sat for a while in silence as if neither felt forced to speak. It was a blessed relief after the hours he'd spent in the gala being solicited by the Minister of Trade. Being peppered with unwanted and intrusive questions that were almost ritualistic in any negotiation. *How are you finding Iondorra? What did you think of the capital Callier? Have you tried some unnameable food the small country hailed as their own pride and joy?* The man's offence that Matthieu had driven here from Switzerland, and intended to drive back without sampling any of this proud nation's delights, had been both clear and disapproving. Not that it mattered—Matthieu hadn't bothered with such things as niceties in a long while. He didn't have to. He was Europe's fourth richest man both in private income and net worth. People came to him.

But not this woman.

'Do you think that there are some things that are unforgivable?' she asked into the night air, without glancing his way.

In truth, he couldn't imagine anything done by a girl who couldn't even drink from a champagne bottle could be unforgivable. However he knew that yes, some things were beyond forgiveness. So he chose his words carefully. 'I think there are two sides to every story.'

She seemed to take this in, as if considering her reply just as carefully.

'I broke up an engagement tonight.'

'Really?' He couldn't help the surprised word that fell from his lips. 'Well, if that's the case, he either wasn't worthy of the engagement, or she wasn't constant in her feelings enough for it.'

'That simple?' she asked of his blunt declaration.

'It usually is, once you take emotions out of it.' He was good at that. He had to be. 'Do you love him?' he asked, genuinely curious.

'I thought I did.'

He knew that feeling too. 'Then he either lied to you, or her.'

'It's not what you think. He had his reasons.'

'They always do.'

'No, I mean…he never… I never…'

He frowned at her confusion, not quite sure what she was unable to put words to.

She turned to him then for the first time and he was struck full force by her beauty. 'What is it like to be kissed?'

He let out a breath he hadn't realised he'd been holding. 'You thought you loved him, but have never been kissed?' he asked, unable to hide the incredulity from his tone.

Perhaps I don't know what love is.

She hadn't said the words out loud in that rich accented tone of hers, but her face was so expressive he could almost read her thoughts. He was used to the practised masks of women hell-bent on seduction. But hers? So open, so revealing, it distracted him for a moment.

Her skin glowed as much as her white lace dress in the beams of the moon. Flawless. Her jaw was strong, angular almost, stubborn even, but drew the eye to perfect rosebud lips slicked with just a trace of something that glistened in the night. Dark brows above dark eyes, highlighted with just a trace of mascara and liner as to outline, rather than dominate the deep rich dark eyes that stared back at him with confusion and hope—and a request he was almost one hundred per cent sure she wasn't aware of.

What is it like to be kissed?

Maria was embarrassed. Should never have asked such a question. Especially not to a man like him. She might not have known who he was—which was partly why she'd felt able to speak her mind—but she didn't have to know his name to know that he *most definitely* knew what it was like to kiss, to touch…to… She yanked her mind back before she could give away her thoughts.

A blush rose almost painfully to her cheeks and she hoped that he might not see it beneath the cover of the night sky. She felt naïve and uncouth next to him. And small. Because…his body, his presence, it was huge. She'd seen the impressive width of his arms as he'd sat down and leaned his weight back on his hands behind him. Arms and muscles that looked too wide for her to encompass with both her hands. If it hadn't been for the champagne bottle, she would have pressed her thighs together against the feeling that was growing within her. She might have been innocent, but she knew the shocking arousal sparking within her was something she rarely felt, even with Theo.

She turned away, but even then, every single feature on his face glowed within her mind. Harsh cheekbones defined by the short beard that covered the strong line of his jaw, framing lips that were almost cruelly sensual. His eyebrows hung low above eyes that were a honey-green shade of hazel, so bright almost that she could have lost herself within their depths.

She thought he wouldn't answer and almost jolted when he did speak.

'There are lots of different types of kisses. Manipulative kisses, to get what you want. Cruel kisses to punish.' Later she would wonder that he chose those two descriptions first. 'Soft, gentle kisses a mother gives her child,' he said, his tone unfathomable and causing a sudden yearning in the pit of her heart. 'Passionate, mindless kisses that are all-consuming, thoughtless and more than a little selfish.'

She turned back to him, startled to find him looking so intently at her. As if trying to figure something out. As if...no. Surely it was only her wondering what it would be like to kiss this man.

'But your first kiss? Honestly? Probably messy and awkward.'

Maria felt a little sad at that. As if somehow he'd taken away the promise of something that would be... good?

'Perhaps I should just get it out of the way, then.'

He huffed out a gentle laugh—not at her, she realised. *With* her. There was a difference.

'Perhaps,' he said ruefully.

'Would you do me a kindness, then? Would you kiss me?'

He met her gaze then, this man whose name she did not even know. And she felt it. That low hum through her body, as if his penetrating stare could reach into the depths of her soul and figure her out, understand her. That was what she'd wanted, she realised. All this time, all these years. Someone to understand. And, having done so, choose to stay.

His eyes roamed her face, looking for what, she didn't know. The hairs on her arms lifted and goosebumps raised across her skin. She resisted the urge to shiver beneath his gaze, because she was scared. Not of him, but of what was happening to her. She'd never wanted something as much as she did his kiss. He frowned for a moment, as if fighting some inner battle she couldn't imagine. He reached out his hand and raised her chin with his finger, looking at her, inspecting her almost.

'Are you sure?'

She nodded, unable to speak. Wondering if he would walk away instead, or give into this strange web woven around them, separating them from the rest of the world.

He moved slowly, as if giving her the chance to turn away, to change her mind. She watched, wide-eyed and fascinated as he bent his head towards her, and… instead of pressing his lips to hers, he passed them, pressing his cheek to hers, stroking it almost, the heat warming her skin and heart, and she heard him breathe in, as if taking her into him, only to finally turn his head back towards her and almost brush a kiss across her lips. Once, then twice.

Her heart soared at the gentle yet firm feel of his lips against hers. Something within her rose to the surface of her skin, clamouring to reach out to him, to feel more than the simple contact of his finger beneath her chin and his lips against hers.

Desperate and fearful that he might pull away, that he might take this away from her, she reached up, inexpertly, to either side of his face, the soft hair of his beard against her palm, her fingers brushing the silky thick strands of his hair. Holding him gently, pulling him back towards her in case he turned away.

His lips hovered barely a centimetre away from hers, she felt his breath against hers, she drew it into her lungs and her stomach clenched as she wished so much that she knew what to do next. Instead, they hovered on this almost kiss, fire scorching through her veins, heart beating so wildly she thought she might never find equilibrium again. Then, as one, they moved, coming together—she opened to the tongue he'd pressed against the seam of her lips and she met it with her own, the first shocking feel of him against her, inside her, filling her and delighting her completely. She lost herself to the kiss, the dance of their bodies, the impossible almost dizzying feeling that consumed her.

She felt his hands in her hair, his fingers curling into the thick tendrils and tightening just a little in a way that strangely made her feel both safe and wanted at the same time. She stretched into the feeling, trying to hold on to each different strand of emotion and desire he was wringing from her with just a kiss.

She couldn't hold back the moan of pure pleasure that fell from her lips to his and regretted it instantly as he finally broke the kiss, his forehead resting against hers, breathing as harshly as she, as if as shocked as she.

'Is it…is it always like that?' she dared to ask.

'No,' he replied darkly. 'Never.'

He took her hand in his, gently pulling it down from the side of his face, his thumb pressing against the palm of her hand soothing a little of the hurt, until it tripped over the scar that stretched over her palm to the top of her wrist. She pulled her hand away, rubbing at the scar with her thumb, not from pain but from the tingles and sparks his touch had created there.

She huffed out a little laugh, disguising her shock from the pleasure he'd just given her.

'My stepmother hates them.'

'What?' he asked as if confused.

She shot a dark look his way. Surely he hadn't missed the callouses, the little scars and nicks around the pads of her fingers, and the larger burn scar that topped the oblique arch of her palm.

'My hands. The scars. She thinks that all well-born ladies should have delicate, unblemished, dainty hands and bathe in milk daily.'

'And sleep on rose petals, I'm sure.'

'And wrap themselves in cotton wool,' she replied, continuing their word game.

'And what do you think?' he asked quietly, as if more weighed on her answer than just her thoughts about herself.

Maria turned her hands over, inspecting them impartially for the first time in a very long time. Seeing them as more than a body part, but as the tools she used to create her jewellery, to meld and mould precious metals, to create beautiful things.

'I think they speak of hard work and sacrifice, hard-earned lessons, and I am proud of every single one of them.'

It was strange to hear her talk of the thing that had blighted so much of his life in a way that was full of pride and defiance rather than disgust or sick fascination. He had certainly met both those reactions. And then there was the other kind. The women who simply viewed what he could give them, in spite of the scars that covered almost half of his torso. The women who were more interested in his wealth or what pleasure he could give them.

'You wouldn't understand,' she said dismissively and he laughed. Properly then, out loud, from deep within him. She turned back to him, curiosity shining in her eyes.

He nodded once, quickly loosening his tie, releasing the button behind it and, moving his head to the side, he pulled slightly at the collar of his shirt. He knew that she would see the tendrils of scars that licked at his neck glinting in the moonlight. Then held out his arm, the same side of his body, and released the cufflink that held his shirt sleeves in place to reveal the edges of the scars that reached from his neck to his wrist.

'I'm sorry.'

As he secured the cufflink, forgoing the button at his neck, he reflected that he'd heard that phrase so many times. From the doctors and nurses who had originally treated him, even from Malcolm. And worse, from the women who decided they couldn't bear to be near him, to touch him. They'd all held *that* tone. Apologetic and, more often than not, disgusted. But this woman's voice held neither of those and for the first time he found himself asking, 'For what?'

'That you feel you have to hide them.'

A jolt passed through his body. No one had ever said that to him. No one had ever accepted his scars so simply and his mind went blank. Well. Almost blank. Because suddenly he was plunged back into the memory of their kiss. He'd not lied when he'd said that a kiss had never been like that for him.

Even now he felt the throb of desire coiled tight within him. His heart was still racing, which had probably accounted for why he had shown her his scars. Perhaps unconsciously he'd been trying to scare her away. Because she was threatening to undo him in a way he'd never experienced before.

'Passionate, mindless kisses that are all-consuming, thoughtless and more than a little selfish.'

His words came back to haunt him and he realised the truth of them. Because it had made him selfish. Her kiss had made him want more, a need rising within him, demanding to be heard and satisfied. *More.* He laughed at himself cynically. He didn't just want more, he wanted it all. Everything she could give him. Need fired his blood, throbbing thick and heavily through his veins. He desperately fought the urge to haul her into his lap and simply feast on her like the beast he was.

'They're from smelting,' she said, cutting through

the raging desire he felt and pulling him back to the present. 'It's—'

'I know what smelting is.' His voice had come out harsher than he'd intended and she had noticed, if her look of confusion was anything to go by. 'Professional interest. Mining.'

She nodded as if that explained everything, including his seven-point-four-billion-dollar net worth that she clearly didn't know about. 'You don't like it though,' she stated.

'I don't like fire.'

'I can't work without it,' she replied, not dwelling on the probable cause of his injuries. She tapped the series of silver bracelets hanging loosely on her wrist. Jewellery. She must make jewellery.

He wished she hadn't said that. Because now there was an image of her taming molten silver, harnessing the power of fire and heat—his greatest foe—and bending it to her will. It would require a greater deal of strength than he'd thought her capable of only ten minutes before. But looking at her now, the pride and innate confidence about her work…her scars even, made her glorious to him.

'One of your own making?'

'Yes. My first piece,' she said lovingly of the simple silver band, not smooth like so many others, but beaten, textured, perfectly imperfect.

Matthieu hadn't realised how strong the cast of light was from the ballroom until it went out. The charity gala had ended and the staff of the hotel had clearly finished their clean up. A brief glance at his watch showed that it was nearly two a.m.

'What are you going to do now?' he asked, almost reluctantly.

She shook her head and shrugged a delicate shoulder. 'Not sure. I can't go back to the suites as my brother will be there and I'm not ready to…' Her rich accented voice trailed off.

'You can't stay out here all night.'

He might be a bastard, but he wasn't that much of a bastard. She had started to shiver as if the gentle light from the hotel behind them had offered both warmth and illumination. He shrugged out of his jacket and placed it around her shoulders, resisting the urge to smooth down the material that swamped her small frame. She smiled her thanks up at him and he cursed the innocence shining in her eyes. If only…

'The hotel is fully booked from the gala. You can have my suite.'

And for the first time that night it was as if his words had broken the spell. There, finally, was that hesitation, that sense of insecurity about his intentions, about him. It was only to be expected, from women who got in over their heads, women who weren't quite ready to 'bed the beast' as he'd heard one such descriptor of himself. She need not worry. He could never touch an innocent such as her.

'You will have it to yourself. Alone,' he concluded firmly.

'What about you?'

'I'll be fine,' he said, standing, firmly tucking his desires and wants for her away. He held out his hand to her. 'Come.'

CHAPTER TWO

MARIA FOLLOWED HIM through the dark halls of the hotel, still clutching the bottle of champagne she had snagged earlier in the evening, thankful that he had his wits about him when hers felt as if they'd fled. Because at first when he'd told her that she could have his suite, she'd been momentarily unsure. But when he had added that she'd have it to herself, alone, she'd been…disappointed.

Which was silly. Even she could recognise that. After all, she'd told him that she'd been in love with another man only hours ago. But Theo had never, *ever*, installed feelings that this man had conjured from her with his presence, his touch…his lips.

She knew she should be ashamed, but she couldn't quite bring the feeling to mind. His impressively broad shoulders took up almost the entire width of the hallway she followed him down, gentle night lighting casting him in shadows. He was huge in comparison to her. Maria didn't usually consider herself small at five foot four, but he must be well over a foot taller than her.

He drew up short at the last doorway at the end of the corridor. Turning to one side, he slid the slim black key card over the electronic plate beneath the handle, pushed the door open and gestured for her to enter.

She stepped past him, registering the oaky cologne that made her think of autumnal woods, earth and something else…something musky and enticing. Her thoughts on that, it took her a moment to recognise the sheer opulence of the room she had entered and she nearly gasped.

Yes, her family might have once been well versed in luxury, but her little flat-share in South London had adjusted her expectations. And this? Plush cream carpets met floor-to-ceiling windows looking out at the stunning night panorama of Lac Peridot, her gaze instantly drawn to where the two opposing mountains met low in the distance.

From the corner of her eye she could make out almost obscenely expensive furnishings and a doorway that presumably led to a bedroom and en suite bathroom, perhaps. But she couldn't tear her eyes away from the view from the windows, just beyond which she could see a small wooden deck with a table and chairs.

She turned, expecting to find him right behind her, *wanting* to even, but instead, she was surprised to find him hovering at the threshold as if reluctant to enter.

'I don't even know your name,' she said, her words a whisper that pitched somewhere between humour and surprise.

'Do you need it?' he asked with a small answering smile curving his lips.

'I'd like to thank you properly.'

'Matthieu.'

She repeated his name, the word rolling off her tongue, shaped by her accent, and read sudden and shocking desire in his eyes as she did so. She felt it. Bound to it, to him. Firing in her a confidence she didn't know that she possessed.

'Thank you, Matthieu.'

He shook his head, dismissing her thanks, and made to turn, but she wasn't ready for him to go. Not yet.

'I—' she said, halting his departure, but also desperately searching for something to say, something to bring him into the suite, to her. 'I told you a secret. Before you go, would you share one with me?'

He frowned then, as if remembering her earlier confession, as if choosing whether to give into her request, and something passed over his features, something hard won.

'What? Like my favourite colour?' he asked, stalking towards her silently on the plush carpet.

'No,' she said, casting her head to one side, taking the entire breadth of him in her gaze. 'It's blue,' she asserted and then smiled when she caught the look of surprise. 'Your suit is deep blue, your watch straps are blue leather.' She shrugged her shoulder.

'That simple?'

'It usually is,' she replied, using his words from earlier that evening. He liked that, she could tell and it warmed her strangely, somewhere beneath her breast bone.

He had reached her and, now that they were standing so close, she had to crane her neck back to look at him. He really was breathtaking, his piercing eyes, a colour similar to rich honey, bearing down into hers.

'It's my birthday,' he said, his voice barely above a whisper, as if it really was a secret to be shared.

'Truly?' she asked as a wide smile pulled at her mouth.

'I don't…usually do celebrations,' he said somewhat distastefully.

She wanted to tell him then that she understood. That she hated her birthday too. But it felt…too personal, too intrusive. His birthday was about him. Not her. She pulled up the bottle of champagne she still clutched, and offered it to him, wondering whether he would take a sip this time.

He gently took the neck of the bottle in his large hands, put it to his lips, making sure there was enough air angled in the throat of the bottle not to funnel the bubbles over him.

But not once did he take his eyes from hers. After he'd taken a mouthful, he passed the bottle back to her and she placed her lips where his had been. The knowledge of it fired her blood once again, bringing a blush to her cheeks and the low v between her breasts. She followed his actions as she took a sip, faintly happy that she didn't end up with a face full of bubbles and look as naïve as she felt in that moment.

She didn't know what she was doing…how to do what she wanted to. And she really wished that weren't the case. Wished, suddenly, for experience to entice, to draw him to her. To know whether it was just her enthralled to this madness.

Matthieu could see it—what her body was asking for—and feared that she wasn't even aware of it. And God help anyone when she became aware of her power. The beauty of this woman could fell armies.

'You know my name,' he stated.

She smiled and nodded her head slowly, understanding the implied question, and delighting in teasing him for it. And surprisingly, he liked it. That teasing sense of her with no emotional undercurrent or ulterior motive. He watched as the teasing morphed into something else…something more primal yet serious.

'Maria. Maria Rohan de Luen.' It was said with a slightly Spanish flare and he mentally rolled it around his mind, liking the way it bounced within him. Unconsciously he mouthed the words, drawing her attention to his lips. The way she looked at his mouth caused that infernal beast within him to roar with pride and need and all the things he knew he should lock down tight. He should not be here. Not tonight, when this woman was threatening his cast-iron defences against things he had not thought of for years.

A timely reminder and one he needed to heed. He nodded once, to himself at his decision made, and then again at Maria, silently bidding her adieu. Because if he didn't leave here soon, he might not leave at all. And she was too pure, too innocent for that. Had never been kissed until this night.

He gave her an almost apologetic smile, the gesture unfamiliar on his lips, and turned to go. He had reached the door, his fingers around the handle before her words stopped him.

'Before you go, can I ask one more thing?'

He turned his head, not a single clue as to what she might ask for. But whatever had run through his mind, it hadn't been what she proceeded to say.

'Would you show me your scars?'

White noise was all he could hear in his mind and below that, somewhere deeper, a furious roar, snarling and gnashing as if some great wound had been re-opened. It must have shown on his face, because Maria took a step back for which he felt instantly regretful. He didn't want her to be scared. But she would be if she saw them. They all were.

Instantly he was transported back to the first time he'd bared himself to a woman. At seventeen, he'd been naïve enough to think that Clara had cared for him. The swift fury that streaked through him at the memory of betrayal had him turning away from Maria.

But…

'I'm sorry.'

'For what?'

'That you feel you have to hide them.'

And why couldn't he show them to Maria? It wasn't

as if he would ever see her again after this night, not once he left this room. She'd found strength and pride in her own scars, but what would she find in his?

'They're not pretty,' he warned.

'I don't care for pretty,' she responded defiantly, not once taking her eyes from his. There was that strength again. The steel that he recognised encased in soft perfection.

Gritting his teeth, he turned and stalked back to her, lifting his shirt from his trousers as he did so. One by one he undid the shirt buttons and still she didn't drop her gaze. The women he usually spent his time with either hungrily sought out the scars that had fuelled his reputation as a beast, or were barely interested in anything above his belt.

Having reached the last button, he took one last look at her before shrugging out of the white shirt and casting it aside, standing there before her unwavering gaze. Maria didn't break the connection between their eyes, not immediately and he gave her credit for that. But finally he closed his eyes, unwilling and unable to see those beautiful features puckered with disgust.

He felt her close the distance between them, the heat from her body pressing against his skin. The *undamaged* skin, because his nerves had been dulled by the injured tissue and skin grafts that covered nearly half of his torso. He felt her circle him, could have sworn he felt the weight of her gaze sparking a thousand starbursts across his body, even the damaged parts. He sensed when she had come back to face him and braced himself as he opened his eyes. But where he had expected revulsion and horror, even the morbid fascination he occasionally experienced, instead he saw wonder and something like awe.

Maria was enthralled. Utterly and completely. *I don't like fire*, that was what Matthieu had said. Yes, his torso had been badly disfigured from the scars that swept around his forearm and reached up to his neck, where she'd seen the silvery traces earlier in the evening. They covered almost half of his chest and, she had seen, wrapped around his flanks and up across his shoulder blades. The twists of tissue, strangely pale, nearly white against his tanned skin, and in some places shiny and criss-crossed from what she could only presume to be many, many skin grafts to help the full thickness burns she could see were from years ago.

The patterns she found on his chest were painfully beautiful to her and she couldn't even imagine the kind of agony he must have experienced for these to heal, nor the time it must have taken. His skin had reformed over the powerful muscles of his arms, just as large as she'd imagined, and the scars rippled over the muscles in his abdomen, the powerful outline of a six pack that spoke to a brutal physical training regime. Because that was what screamed at her most as he stood there, shirtless, his lower limbs encased in low-slung blue superfine trousers. Strength and raw power. Power that was almost straining at some kind of self-imposed leash.

'What do you see?' he asked. Demanded almost.

And she said the words that had come to her mind. 'Magnificence.' *Raw masculinity*, but she couldn't let herself say that last out loud. Because it spoke too much to her desire for him. It would have betrayed her.

She reached out a hand, but he caught it in the air between them. His large fingers wrapping easily, firmly but gently, around her slim wrist.

She threw her gaze to his, aware that her breath had hitched in her lungs. Aware that her skin was on fire as surely as his had once been. But hers was an invisible flame, one created by him and the need to feel his skin against the palm of her hand. Not from curiosity, but the desperation to make that connection. To feel that same incredible sensation she had experienced when they had kissed earlier. And then she realised to her shame how selfish that was. Just as he'd said earlier about passion. But it was more than that. She wanted to be with him, to soothe that ragged sense of…of… she couldn't put a name to what she saw in his eyes.

She pressed past her hand, still clasped in his, and closed the distance between their bodies. He held himself still, but she could see what an effort that took and she was torn…torn between recognising the stress he put himself under and the need to offer consolation. Instinct won out and she pressed a gentle kiss to his chest, on his pectoral muscle that had the twist and turn of a scar that had shaped itself in such a way that made her think of a great white oak tree, gnarled but majestic.

She traced the trail her lips covered across his chest with her free hand, delighting in the hitch in his breathing as cruel as it was. Because she wanted him with her in this. As utterly devastated and destroyed by the attraction that flamed between them. Though she was innocent, she could recognise the desire in his eyes, recognise it because she felt it within herself.

Pressing another kiss in the centre of his chest, she felt oddly exposed, wanting his arms to wrap around her, hide her from the passion that was almost overwhelming her. He was so broad that she realised only lower around his waist would her arms meet were she to encircle him. But one hand was still captured by his, and the rapid rise and fall of Matthieu's chest was the only outward sign that he was not made of stone.

No. This man would never have been made of stone...pure silver, she thought, only just tempered, still seething with heat from the furnace, still malleable, but just as dangerous. A quiver of desire racked her body and only then did Matthieu finally release her hand. She looked up into eyes that were boring down into hers.

'Stop.'

'Why?'

'You don't know what you're doing. What you're asking for,' he stated, almost angrily.

'I may be naïve—'

'Maybe? You are an innocent, Maria. A true innocent.'

'Does that mean I don't know what I want?'

'It means you don't understand the *implications* of what you want.'

'Would anyone?' she asked.

'This is something that you should do with someone capable of staying with you.'

No one ever stays, her mind voiced, batting away each and every one of his arguments. She knew, deep down, that this was what she wanted with her entire being. She had never been more sure of anything, half fearful that if he walked away now she would have lost something that she had only dreamed of in the darkest of nights and the deepest of sleeps.

'I haven't asked for anything more than this night.'

Matthieu had been wrong. She *was* a seductress. A temptress. Offering him something he could barely stand to walk away from. She was so beautiful, so pure…the light to his darkness and he would drag her down with him if he gave her what she wanted.

I haven't asked for anything more than this night.

He had never allowed himself to take anything so pure. His chosen bedfellows were ones who understood. Who knew the game. Pleasure to be given and received and nothing more. Because he had learned long ago that anything more was a foolish dream. And he refused to be the one to teach Maria that lesson.

But he couldn't help the thought that if he turned away now, if he left her alone, it might break something deep within him.

He shut that thought down as quickly as it had formed in a mental move practised over many years. What he was considering was madness. But then she pressed another kiss to his chest and everything in him was plunged into thick swathes of desire and need, and he felt the growl start at the back of his throat, desperate to stifle it before it escaped into the room.

'Please?' she asked between the infernal kisses she was drawing on his body, his skin, the places usually specifically avoided by others.

'Don't you see, Maria? You shouldn't have to beg for this.'

'I am not begging, I am asking. This is my choice. My request. Stay with me, just for this night. Please.'

And finally Matthieu lost the battle. The battle against being decent, walking away and leaving Maria untouched. Because he could stand it no longer. He wanted to touch her, feel her smooth skin, so pale against his it seemed almost to glow. He wanted to tease pleasure from her so much that it was almost a physical ache within him. Finally he was about to live down to his reputation as a beast in the truest sense, because he felt the last vestige of restraint burn to dust beneath her lips.

This time he was unable to stifle the growl that rose in the back of his throat, as he wrapped his arms around her, drawing her to him and feasting on her lips as he'd wanted to from that very first moment.

This was no practised, gentle first kiss, this was desire, desperation even, as he plunged the depths of her mouth with his tongue, drawing little mewls of pleasure from her. Her hands, now free, swept into his hair, pulling him further down towards her. Not enough, he thought, it was nowhere near enough.

He lifted her up, so that her legs wrapped around his waist, and her lips met his, until finally he nudged her head aside and found the delicate, smooth arc of her neck and pressed open-mouthed kisses against her skin, lathing it with his tongue. Maria's head fell back, exposing the pale column of her neck and the v of her perfect breasts, accentuated by the silver necklace dipping between them.

He marvelled at how light she was. He could have held her there for an eternity. But her body shifted restlessly in his arms, wanting more, demanding it. She might have not known the words, but her body knew the moves, instinct driving them closer together in their need.

He carried her through to the bedroom, not once breaking the contact between his lips and her skin. As he placed her on the edge of the bed, he cursed. Her pupils so large her eyes were almost completely black, she was drunk on desire.

'Are you sure?'

'Never more so,' she said with a faint smile, faint only because the rest of her features were a mask of pure need and want.

'I need you to understand that you can stop this at any time. *Any* time.'

'You want me to give you a safe word?'

He barked a laugh at the mock coquettishness in her tone. 'No, I don't want a bloody safe word.' The sudden and surprising humour delighting him and, from the look in her eyes, Maria too. As if somehow she'd known they needed a moment, a brief respite from the all-consuming passion that had driven them this far. 'What do you know of safe words?' he queried.

'I may be innocent, but I'm not naïve.'

He dragged in a lungful of air, looking at her in the half light of the moon, cast through the large windows fronting the entire side of the room. Her white lace dress hanging low on her shoulders, exposing collarbones so enticing, he couldn't resist.

He leaned forward, Maria shifting her legs apart to give him room, and placed kisses there, his lips meeting the hard bone covered in soft skin and sucking gently. He pulled back only to place his forehead against hers.

'I want you to know that you can say "no", at any point. I want you to be *able* to say it.'

'I don't want you to stop, Matthieu. I want you to kiss me. To touch me, to—'

He couldn't take any more of her desires, he was battling enough of his own, so he stifled her words with a kiss. Her lips opened for him, offering him entry and damnation at the same time.

He gently pulled at the thin lace of the dress, exposing the smooth pale planes of her chest, the silver necklace she wore a guide line as he leaned her back against the soft bed and kissed his way towards her breasts. The rosy tips stark against the gleaming white skin. He took one in his mouth, his tongue sweeping over the stiff peak, drawing a moan of pleasure from her body and bringing her closer, pressing into his mouth instinctively.

In one hand he fisted the lacy material of her dress, drawing the material tight against her leg. She was glorious in her pleasure and he reached for her thigh, bringing it up on the bed, and feeling the length of her calf, the smoothness of her thigh, more. He wanted more.

Releasing his hold on the delicate lace he'd bunched around her waist, he pressed kisses against the plane of her skin where her hip dipped naturally, leading him to the flat stretch of her stomach, as he gently pressed her thigh to the side with one hand and drew her white panties down with the other to expose the dark curls between her legs.

He cradled her backside in one hand, gently pulling her body towards his, as he slipped the silky material down her thighs and away from her ankles. He ignored the slight tremor of his hands, the almost painful arousal pressing against the seam of his trousers, as he spread her before him and bent forward to taste, to delight in the secret heart of her. The taste of her sweet wet heat was almost too much for him to bear, but he would. He wanted to give her every pleasure she could experience.

Maria was shaking. Never before had she felt anything like this. Pleasure so acute and so extreme, she trembled, a thin sheen of sweat breaking out across the back of her neck. Her hips bucked against the exquisite torture his tongue was wringing from her body and she bit her hand to prevent the cry of sheer pleasure that wanted to escape from her lips. The other fisted the sheets of the bed, anchoring herself to something, anything, before her body threatened to drift away on a tide of pleasure so powerful she feared she might never return.

Rolling waves covered her body, as if desperately trying to reach the shore, but not quite, not yet. Again and again they bit at the edge of her body, threatening to drag her under. Then Matthieu threaded a finger deep within her, the pressure inside her coiling tight, her body unconsciously trying to hold him within her.

Her pleas became unintelligible demands, her breathing both desperate and stifled at the same time, her body on the brink of something she couldn't quite define, waves ebbing and flowing faster and faster until…

The orgasm he had wrung from her body plunged her deep beneath the surface of the water, the pounding waves now all she could hear as her body shook and shuddered, soothed only when she felt Matthieu's arms come around her, cocoon her in his embrace, keeping her safe and anchored to him while her soul soared towards the night sky.

As if on a string tied to him, her mind returned to the man surrounding her, caging her as if trying to keep out the night, the dark…the morning perhaps. Her arms reached around his trim waist, feeling along the powerful muscles bracketing his hips, and meeting the soft midnight-coloured material of his trousers. They were still clothed, she both marvelled and regretted. She wanted to feel him, all of him, against her skin, without barriers. Her hands sought out the fastening of his trousers and he shifted as if realising her intention.

Matthieu leaned back, almost regretting the loss of contact. For the first time ever he had found something like peace in her pleasure, in offering something of himself to another. But one look at the determined jut of her jaw, the challenge in her eyes daring him to ask her if she might want to stop, ironically only fuelled his need for her, as yet unquenched and unsatisfied.

Slowly he reached for the button of his trousers, gliding the zip down and loosening the stranglehold the material had on his crotch. His erection jutted free as he swept his trousers and underwear over his hips, down his legs, and kicked them away.

He watched and waited as she took in the sight of him, the unconscious way her tongue curved over her bottom lip and the teeth that plunged into the soft, wet pink flesh. He groaned again at the effect she had on him and his heart almost stopped as she reached for the hem of her white lace dress and pulled it up, over her thighs and hips, over her chest and head, casting it to some distant part of the room. She was glorious, her legs bent at the knee, sitting up, only her hands fisting the sheets of the bed giving expression to the barely leashed desire he felt meeting his own.

He reached into his wallet and retrieved the packet,

tearing the foil with his teeth, not once taking his eyes from her. He watched her eyes grow wide with fascination as he rolled the condom over his length, her gaze glancing between his face and his erection, and if he'd had any doubts as to her certainty, the way she parted her legs, making room for him as he came down between them, burned them from his mind.

He leaned to support his weight on one elbow, the fingers of his free hand dipping and tripping over the skin from the centre of her collarbone, following the silver lines of her necklace down the irresistible v between her breasts, and over the gentle swell of her abdomen. Maria's body gently shivered in the wake of his fingers and he couldn't help but press his lips to the centre of her chest. Her hands swept to either side of his face, fingers splaying in his hair and nails gently scraping against his scalp. He leant into her touch, kissing her wrist, and finally turned back to her watchful gaze.

A slight nod was all he needed from her as he gently pressed into her, forcing himself to go slowly despite how everything roared within him for instant completion. The damp wet heat of her surrounding him was so incredible it rendered him mindless, but not heedless, as he felt her stiffen beneath him, bringing an instant halt to his movements.

The hitch in her breath, the slight frown to her brows, through which he held his breath. If she wanted him to stop he'd do it. It might kill him, but he'd do it. But she didn't. She looked into his eyes, as if understanding the battle that waged within him, a small smile pulling at the curve of her lips. 'Please?'

'Please what, Maria? Because—'

'Don't stop. Please don't stop.'

Her hand swept around his neck and pulled him to her, into her kiss, into her more deeply and into an insatiable madness he didn't know he'd survive. Slowly he began to move, his hips gently driving into her depths, feeling her completely encase him, and he wondered somewhere if this was what he'd been missing his entire life. Her.

Maria's breaths became faster, her moans, full of pleasure and need, filled the air between them. Her hips raised against his, holding him within her, deeper and longer… The rhythm *she* was setting, *she* was dictating, one that only fired his blood and his arousal to a point where he didn't know whose heartbeat he could feel in his chest.

He reached beneath her and drew her closer to him, his chest pressed against hers, inhaling the sweet scent of her at the edge of her neck, the soft curls of her long hair tickling the skin on his chest. Soon thought became ephemeral, words intangible, and all he knew was her and the exquisite feeling of losing himself within her depths. Need and arousal became his oxygen and he inhaled it like a drowning man, intoxicated by her, lost to her.

As he felt her tighten around him, heard the way her breath hitched at its highest point, he knew they were both on the edge, on the brink, and one final thrust of his hips saw them cut their ties to the night and melt away.

Through the night hours, between sleep and waking, they reached for each other, finding pleasure, seeking more, and as the sun's early morning rays tripped into the room Maria spread her arm out behind her feeling only the cool silky sheets beneath her palm. Matthieu had done what he'd promised. Given her one night and then…left.

CHAPTER THREE

MARIA SHIFTED ON the seat to relieve the pins and needles that were creeping around the base of her spine. Her knee tapped an incessant rhythm, partly because after three and a half hours of sitting there, she really needed to go to the bathroom.

The foyer of the office building in Switzerland was immaculate—all concrete and steel—but faintly cold in the encroaching evening's darkness. The silver letters of Montcour Mining rose high above the reception desk she'd not been allowed to pass. Her knee bobbed away, which the blond haired male receptionist misunderstood and took as a sign of impatience.

She'd studied every inch of the two large canvasses bracketing the broad wooden-fronted desk. Rothko. In all probability real rather than reproduction. She deduced this not from the fine artistry, but more from the research she had done to discover Matthieu's last name and location.

It had been three months since she'd seen him. Two since she'd started to feel the waves of nausea that had completely taken her by surprise. One month since one little blue line had changed her life for ever, and only a few days since she'd had the first scan that truly confirmed that her life—*their* lives—had changed for ever.

Maria had thought she'd have to spend hours trawling through reams of pages on the Internet and had already considered reaching out to Princess Sofia, who had patronised the charity where Maria had met Matthieu for a list of attendees that night. Having reunited with Theo, Sofia had forgiven Maria for her indiscreet argument with Theo. It had been swept under the carpet with happiness and love that shined from the couple on their wedding day.

In the past, thinking of such a thing would have brought her the sharp agony of unrequited love—but that was before Matthieu and before… Her hand unconsciously swept over her abdomen. She avoided another glare from the frustrated receptionist, by focusing on the beautiful modern chandelier suspended from a ceiling that rose at least ten stories high. The lights fiercely illuminating the space, yet tempered and golden hued to soften the impact on the eye. The building screamed money. But then when a person was as wealthy as Matthieu Montcour it could be afforded.

She supposed that many would have considered themselves lucky to be tied to such a wealthy man. She was not one of those people and instead was more concerned about how *he* might feel being tied to *her*.

She had left his suite in Iondorra that morning and returned to find a furious Sebastian ready to read her the Riot Act for disappearing the night before. But he'd taken one look at her and when she had asked to go home, he'd relented and taken her back to her flat-share in South London.

For a month she had lost herself in days full of work, her jewellery making and her part-time coffee-shop job. But her nights? They were lost to dreams of Matthieu and the pleasure he'd wrung from her body.

In Camberwell, the daily reality of her life trudged on and he became something almost mythical to her, fantastical and almost imagined. She'd not said a word about him to Anita, or Evin, her two flatmates, who she'd met in the first week of her Foundation Course.

After the staunchness of her Italian schooling, Camberwell had been both a breath of fresh air and truly liberating. She fell hard for the heady mix of cultures, the strange juxtaposition of houses worth millions and council estates worth almost nothing. She felt as if it suited her life, having known both sides, extreme wealth and sudden shocking poverty after her father's near bankruptcy and subsequent exile from Spain.

She risked a glance at the imperious receptionist banging away on a keyboard as if it might make her disappear. But Maria wasn't going anywhere.

One month ago, after the third week of being unable to hold in her nausea, Anita had handed her a pregnancy test, given her a small smile, a pat on the arm, a cup of tea—so very English—and left her to it. Maria barely remembered the following two days. She had been numb with shock and battered by so many unanswered and unanswerable questions, and only one thought had remained constant. Remained true.

I'm keeping the baby.

She promised herself that once she reached three months, once she'd had her first scan, only then would she tell Matthieu.

The clipped sound of stiletto heels machine-gun-fired across the marble foyer, drawing Maria into the present. An obscenely glamorous woman in an ankle-length wool coat with a fur trim swept an about-turn to face a trio of sheepish-looking men in suits.

'That man is absolutely impossible. No wonder they call him a beast.' The last word was hissed, as if to be conveyed in a whisper, but rang like a bell.

Maria had no doubt as of whom she was speaking. Not after her Internet search of Matthieu. She'd had two words. His name, and mining—his 'professional interest'. She hadn't held up much hope, but she'd been wrong. A second after she'd hit enter, the screen had filled with the image of his face—a stern headshot, his piercing golden eyes so intense she'd felt a blush rise to her cheeks as if he could see her searching for him.

'No wonder he's as rich as Croesus, when he's that tight-fisted with his business interests.'

Maria had discovered that too. Reportedly he was the fourth richest man in Europe. And it had shocked her. Clearly he had been wealthy, must have been to gain entry to the gala, but reports stated that his net worth was near eight billion. *Billion.*

But it had come at such a terrible cost. She'd gasped as she'd read descriptions of the fire that had not only consumed the estate where Matthieu had lived as a child, but also his entire family. The one that had caused the scars she'd felt beneath the soft palm of her hand, hard and twisted, but somehow also defiant and magnificent. The sheer number of articles on the years of treatments was surpassed only by the fascination with the shocking amount of the life insurance heaped upon an eleven-year-old boy, making him unimaginably wealthy independent of his family's business. Maria's heart had broken at the grainy images from years ago of the small boy accompanied by his, then, legal guardian following behind five coffins: his parents, two uncles and one aunt. She couldn't even conceive how devastating that must have been.

As the woman swirled back towards the exit, taking the suits and the drama with her, Maria was dragged into the present and stifled a wave of nausea as the woman's sickly perfume reached her on the ruffled air.

The receptionist cleared his throat and stood, apparently having reached the end of his patience at housing the unwanted and uninvited guest in his domain.

'I'm afraid I'm going to have to ask you to—'

'Maria?'

Her head turned to the bank of elevators tucked off to the right of the reception desk to see Matthieu Montcour looking as shocked as she suddenly felt at seeing him in the flesh again after twelve weeks.

Matthieu watched her spring up from the sofa she'd been sitting on, a bundle of energy in the almost silent reception.

'Where's your bathroom?' she asked breathlessly, her tone betraying her desperation.

'It's—'

'I'm sorry, this isn't how I wanted this to go, it's just that I really...' she did a little dip as if to punctuate her need '...*really* need the bathroom. Please don't go anywhere, we need to talk, it's just that I need the—'

'Bathroom. Got it. Round the corner on the left,' he said, gesturing with his arm.

She ran, literally ran around the corner, skidding a little on her boot heels as she rushed through the doors.

And he couldn't help but laugh. A sound startling to his own ears, let alone his stiff receptionist.

He shook his head, trying to jolt himself free from the effect of her sudden and shocking appearance. It wasn't as if he hadn't thought of her in the last three months, thought of finding her, his fingers itching to type her name into the search engine on his computer. In truth, there hadn't been a day—or night—that he hadn't remembered her soft sighs, or the feel of her beneath him. The wrenching he'd felt that morning after, when he'd sneaked out of the room, leaving her asleep in the bed of his suite. Both hating himself and knowing that it was right.

But why was she here? What did she want?

Then a cold steel clamp choked his thoughts.

She knew. Who he was.

And just like so many women before him, Maria had come to cash in on his notoriety. Had thought to play on the vulnerabilities he'd accidentally exposed that night. The one night he'd offered her and no more.

Anger clenched his jaw. He had thought her different. He had thought her to be something…almost mythical in her purity. A purity that he had single-handedly taken that night. He should have known better. Had he not learned at seventeen what the female sex wanted from him?

The sound of her boots on the marble floor cut through his thoughts and he turned to find her looking up at him nervously, her hands twisting within each other, but valiantly bearing the weight of his scrutiny as he searched her expressive features for clues of her motivation for being here.

She was still breathtakingly beautiful. He'd half convinced himself that he'd imagined it. The shocking impact she'd had on him that night. The way that his pulse kicked up a notch, just being near her. The way his need rose within him to seize him by the throat.

'Hi,' she said simply.

He nodded, unable to trust himself to say more. To bring about the moment where she exposed her greed.

'Can we…?'

'Talk?'

She nodded, an almost sad smile on her features. And for a moment he almost felt sorry for her. Because while she obviously knew who he was, she clearly did not realise just who she was up against.

'This way,' he said, his words as clipped as the sound of their shoes as he led them to the last elevator.

He swiped his key card over the electronic plate and the doors swished apart revealing the mirror-lined lift that led only to the top floor where his offices were housed.

She silently followed him into the confined space and when he inhaled he was swamped by that scent of hers. Sage and salt, something so unique to her and that night that he had to fight against the sudden wave of desire that rose up within him from being this close to her.

He studied her in the mirrors, Maria determinedly looking ahead and not making eye contact, offering him the chance to take in her appearance. The night they'd met, she had been dressed in white lace. Now, she wore tight grey denim jeans and a black leather waterfall jacket that covered a loose T-shirt in a burnt-pink colour.

Her hair, loose again, fell in waves over her shoulders and down her back, the slight curls twisting strands of dark browns and reds, making him want to reach out and touch. But he stifled the ridiculous urge.

The elevator drew to a stop and the doors opened, prompting him to gesture for her to go first, and then he realised how silly that was, when she pulled up short in the large area between three glass-fronted rooms. Two of which were meeting rooms, the third, his office.

He stepped around her and entered the latter. Immediately regretting not showing her to one of the large meeting rooms and ensuring that she would be ill at ease and more likely to reveal the truth about her intentions under such stark surroundings.

Instead, his office was completely different. Dark brown leather sofas faced each other, with a corner chair bracketing the end nearest the side wall. A discreet unit fronted the rest of the wall on the other side of a hidden door in the panelling that led to a bathroom and shower unit. A fireplace was hidden by the large corner chair—one that he never used and tried as much as possible to ignore behind the smooth dark leather. His father had loved it when this office had been his and, as much as he'd wanted to brick it up, he couldn't seem to do so.

The opposite wall, in front of which was his desk, was covered head to toe in shelves full of books. Beautiful leather-spined tomes that gave the room an almost gothic feel, despite the sleek modern technology that covered the desk. Two large monitors fed into a discreet desktop hidden on a lower-level shelf just beneath the surface of the desk—a feature that had forced him to raise the desk a few inches in order to seat his long legs comfortably and without taking his kneecaps off every time he sat.

He turned to watch Maria take in the space.

'Would you care for a drink?' he asked, his hands unaccountably reaching for the bottle of whisky that had remained largely untouched for the three years it had been in his office's wet bar.

'Sparkling water, please.'

Where had the woman so full of words and even a bit of humour gone? Perhaps it was him. Was she picking up on his cynical reaction to her presence?

He poured sparkling water over ice, the cubes splintering and fracturing beneath the liquid in each glass. He passed Maria's drink to her and was about to say some pithy salutation when she blurted, 'I'm pregnant.'

The glass hovered before his lips, his fingers gripping it so hard, his knuckles turned white from his apparent shock. His eyes went from speculative to furious in a heartbeat and Maria inwardly cursed, wishing she'd had the courage to say it more gently, to warn him… Anything other than what she'd just thrown between them like an unexploded bomb. Only it wasn't unexploded. It had detonated three months earlier, though neither of them had known.

'Congratulations. Who is the lucky man?'

Maria frowned, both shocked and confused by his question.

'What do you mean?' she said, wondering why she was still holding the glass of water and he his, as if they were having a polite exchange rather than the fact he'd just implied that…that…

'Well, given that we used protection, *every single time*—'

'Wait, what?'

'You cannot really expect to turn up here a convenient three months after our…encounter, and lay claim to my being the father of this miraculous child?'

She was speechless. She had imagined this conversation so many times, but this? Not what she'd expected. Encounter? He'd called the night they shared an *encounter*? Now she was angry. Of all the feelings she'd experienced thus far, since discovering the fact she was to have a child, anger had not been one of them. Until now.

'You bastard.'

'I think the press prefer to call me a beast, but I suppose that will do just as well.'

'I shouldn't have come here,' she said, more to herself, rather than him. But it didn't stop him from answering.

'No, you probably shouldn't have,' he said, sighing as if she were an inconvenience rather than the mother of his child. 'Many others have tried to lay claim to such a thing, and believe me, Maria, they were much more skilled at deception than you. And ultimately, they were proved to be the lying, scheming serpents that they were. I must say, I'm quite disappointed. I had thought you different.'

Maria shook her head. Both at the shocking hostility in his tone and at the awfulness that there had been women who had apparently tried to trick him in the past. In a second, all the things she thought they'd shared, the beauty of that one night she'd clung to as her world had morphed and changed before her eyes, burned to dust. She didn't know this man. She was nothing to him. And she would never, *never*, force such a thing upon her child.

'Not as disappointed as I am. I hope that your conscience is kind to you when you realise just how wrong you are,' she stated, gathering her wits about her, and the scraps of her feelings from the floor. She placed the untouched glass down on the small coffee table, reaching into her bag to retrieve the black and white sonogram image of their, no *her*, child—the one thing that she could give him, the only thing, and, placing it beside the glass, she turned her back on him and stepped towards the door.

'Wait.'

'What for?' she asked without turning, her back still to him. 'For you to hurl even more insults at me? I don't think so.'

'Please.'

She turned then, not because his tone was pleading—which it wasn't—but because she would give him this chance. She needed to. She found him standing by the coffee table, one finger on the corner of the sonogram. He wasn't looking at her, but at it. The image of their child. She wondered what he saw in the grey shapes, the patches of darkness and the surprisingly detailed white figure of their baby. The head, the umbilical cord, arms and legs, all clearly visible.

Finally he looked up at her.

'Do not lie to me about this, Maria. Do not test me.'

She shook her head. 'I'm not. I'm pregnant. The baby is yours.'

'How?'

Again, shaking away the doubt and confusion she had felt when she'd first seen that thin blue line. 'Condoms aren't fail proof, I wasn't on any other kind of contraception. I...' She shrugged.

'You're pregnant. The baby is mine.'

* * *

Maria nodded and Matthieu's whole world shifted on its axis. He cast his eye back to the small black and white image on the coffee table. His child?

'I'm…' stunned, shocked…what? His mind was completely blank. Though the one thing he could recognise above the white noise roaring in his ears was that Maria deserved an apology.

'I'm sorry,' he said, the sea of confusion and chaotic thoughts making his tone dark, guttural almost. The instant refusal that had risen to his mind had been both cruel and devastating. He hadn't missed the way her already pale skin had turned almost bone white beneath his taunt. But it hadn't been that that had convinced him that she spoke the truth. No. It had been her ready departure. So different from the crocodile tears and insincere desperation he'd experienced in the past. Maria had been willing to walk away not just from him, but from what many others had tried to secure. His money. His ring.

A ring he'd once sworn never to put on a woman's finger. Never imagining for a second the need to do so. Never being so unfailingly irresponsible to sire a child that would, along with its mother, invade his carefully ordered life.

He gestured for her to sit and only after she had stiffly approached the sofa opposite where he stood, and sat, or rather collapsed slightly into the deeply upholstered leather, did he finally sit down too.

'What is it you want?' he asked, holding her gaze

with the steel trap of his own, ruthlessly seeking out her intentions, almost willingly seeing hints of her avarice.

'Nothing,' she said, seemingly confused by his question. 'I just wanted to let you know. You...have that right.'

He bit back a cynical laugh. He doubted the truth of her words very much. She might not be after his money or his ring, but there must be something. There was always something.

'You waited three months?' he said, accusingly, not having to work hard to do the maths. He'd known every single one of the days since he'd last touched her, kissed her, brought them both to orgasm.

She nodded. 'The first three months are so...precarious,' she said, shaking her head and shoulders, as if she hadn't been alone to bear the weight of that knowledge, that fear that something could have happened, could have taken away their...their child.

The child he could see formed by light and dark in the small black and white sonogram on the table between them.

'Did you think that I would try to change your mind? Is that why you waited?' Not needing to work hard to find the fury at the possibility that she would think such a thing of him.

'It wouldn't have mattered. I'm keeping this baby, Matthieu, whether you want to be part of its life or not.'

'I would never—'

'How would I know that?' she demanded. 'I didn't even know your last name.'

'But you found out.' The unspoken question in his mind rang loud, beating in time with his heart.

'Only when I needed to.' Her assurance, the promise offered by her words that she had not sought him out until she'd had to, melted the ire edging his anger, transforming it, lessening it—but only slightly. 'Look, I respected what you said then about it only being one night,' she pressed on. 'I'm only here now to let you know, and to give you the chance to choose whether you would like to be in the baby's life or not. Nothing more, nothing less.'

'That simple?' he asked, unconsciously echoing the conversation from that night.

'I am beginning to see that where you are concerned, Matthieu, nothing is simple.'

He reached then for his water, not because he was thirsty, but to buy time. And he never had to buy time. He always knew what to say, how to react. Until now. Until her. He began to wonder if he ever had any choice in the matter at all. His body overriding all senses, all sensibilities.

Father.

He was going to be a father.

'We will marry.'

The look on her face would have been comical in any other circumstance. The horror and shock overriding the fierce neutrality that she had presented in the last few moments.

'No.'

That's different. So many had tried to coerce themselves into his life, but of course Maria was different. He briefly wondered if this might have been part of some larger game, some grander scheme, but he decided not. There had been nothing about Maria then, or now, that indicated some ulterior motive. Wasn't that what had driven him to her in the first place? Her innocence?

'I don't think you understand—'

'No. It is you who doesn't understand,' Maria cut in. 'That's not why I came here. I have no intention of marrying you. I don't want that, or your money. My *only* interest is the level of your involvement in my child's—'

'Our child's,' he said, interrupting her.

'Our child's life.'

'And that is what I'm telling you, Maria. My interest will be deep, my level of involvement will be total.'

CHAPTER FOUR

MARIA FELT PULLED beneath a tide of emotion, some parts fear, some parts daunted, and all parts consuming. She hadn't lied to him. She hadn't come here to demand marriage, or anything more than maybe weekend visits. She hadn't imagined that he'd even want that if she was honest. Certainly not after reading the hundreds of articles on the 'notorious beast'. She hated herself for using that description even mentally. Because she knew why they had called him that. His scars had made him the subject of intense speculation, his wealth and almost cruel single-minded, driven success all the more so.

And now, to have all that focus pinned on her... She couldn't help but want to shrink back from it. But she couldn't. Not now that she had someone else to protect. Her unborn child. Her hands instinctively wrapped around her waist, his hawk-eyed gaze watching her every move.

'Why?' she couldn't help but ask. Everything about Matthieu screamed isolation. The way he did his business, the way he reportedly lived.

'I will protect my child,' he said, his determined voice sending a shiver down her back.

'Protect? Not love?' she demanded. Because in truth that was all that mattered to Maria right now. It was the only thing that mattered.

'Of course I will love my child,' he said dismissively. *But not the mother of his child.*

Maria pushed aside the sad thought. How had this happened to her? Just when she was on the brink of her freedom, her jewellery business beginning to find traction, her false feelings for Theo behind her, to discover who she was outside that, to find an independence that meant so much to her.

'We don't have to marry for you to…protect our child.'

He scoffed an almost cruel laugh. 'Are you that naïve, Maria? Do you have even an inkling of what will happen when the press find out?'

She hadn't thought of that. She simply hadn't thought of anything past the point of telling Matthieu about the baby. Unease began to grow within her at the sheer conviction in his tone.

'They will hound you, Maria. They will dig up every little thing they can find out about you. They will stalk your friends and family, they will offer money for any salacious story they could print, they will go through your rubbish and camp on your doorstep. They will follow you and anyone who knows you.'

Maria didn't have to work hard to imagine the awful things he was saying. Because she knew how the press worked. Had experienced a little of it first hand when her father had been exiled, when her brother had been forced to assume the purse strings and sell off nearly every single thing they had owned. Even now they still stalked Sebastian and every single woman he encountered. Some thought he courted it, but Maria knew he resented it, hated it. But he was happy as long as they'd left her alone.

Her brother. Her protector. Just as Matthieu wanted to protect their child. She didn't think for a minute that Seb could help her in this situation though. No. The Rohan de Luens were minor exiled nobility. Matthieu Montcour was a completely different level of notoriety and fame. She had seen that for herself within seconds of hitting enter on the search bar with his name in it.

His words had conjured exactly what he had intended. Fear. And more than that. His words had chipped away at her belief that she could still have her freedom, that she could still be in charge of her life the way she hadn't before now, and now never would.

'But *how* can we marry? I don't know anything about you,' she said, fighting back the rising tide of panic in her chest.

'You know my birthday and my favourite colour. That is more than most know.'

'You don't know anything about me,' she said, almost on a whisper as her last defences began to crumble. He waited until she met his gaze before speaking and his words were the final blow.

'I know that you make jewellery and that you do it in

spite of your stepmother's objections. I know that you are kind and thoughtful or you wouldn't have been so upset at the idea of breaking someone's engagement, no matter how you thought you felt about the groom. I know that you are not after my money or this conversation would have been significantly different, and I know that you are strong, defiant and determined. And I *know* that you will do whatever you need to do to protect our child.'

I also know the feel of your skin beneath mine, the blush that rises to your cheeks when you can't fight your desires, and I know the sounds of your pleasure when you climax, Matthieu concluded silently, unwilling to speak his wayward thoughts out loud.

He watched as her eyes grew wide with surprise, a faint blush—as if conjured by his very thoughts—rising to her cheeks.

'If we were to marry… *If,*' she repeated as if she hadn't already made her decision, which he very much believed that she had. 'What would that…be like? What would it look like to you?'

Terms. He was good at this. Securing contracts and finalising practicalities. He would have time later to consider the implications of impending fatherhood. Feelings had no place here, not now. The irony of that would have struck a more righteous man in the heart.

'You will live with me here in Switzerland. I can arrange for everything you could ever need to be available to you. As I'm sure you have already figured out, there are certainly benefits to marrying me. Especially for your business.'

'No. That's…that's not up for discussion. My business is mine and I don't want your involvement.'

He frowned. For many, that would have been enticement enough.

'I have contacts around the world and the resources to give you access to some of the finest materials—'

'I said no. I can source my own materials and any achievements I make professionally will be my own.'

Her words were fast and harsh, as dark as he'd ever heard her tone, both tonight and three months ago. Clearly her independence was important to her, but he resisted the urge to warn her not to let pride get in the way of success. Partly because he very much found pride in his own success. He knew what that meant and found that he respected her for it.

'Do you have a particular stipulation in mind?'

He also gave her credit for not flinching, though clearly she wanted to. It might have been distasteful to discuss the matter in such a way, but necessary to avoid future upset, misunderstandings…he couldn't say heartache, because he would never, *never*, allow himself such an indulgence.

'I…we…would stay married until our child is at least twenty.'

He almost laughed then, at her naivety, her innocence. 'Maria, hear this now. In the little time they were alive, my parents at least installed in me a sense of the sanctity of marriage. I may not be religious, but I do not believe in divorce.'

As if refusing to acknowledge his declaration, she looked at her hands.

'I'm not sure that I can just pack up my life and move in with you.'

'Really? I get the impression that you are more than capable of anything you put your mind to, Maria.'

Her gaze flew to his and her expressive face registered surprise, and something else…something warmer, serving only to heat his blood from within. He ruthlessly pushed that aside. It was absolutely vital that he got her agreement in this. He'd meant what he said. He would protect his child, and by extension her too. But he wouldn't lie to her. She had asked him of his expectations and it was important that he state his intentions now.

'My home is on the edges of Lake Lucerne, in the heart of this country. It is…certainly big enough for us, and our child.' He knew his words were modest. The large sprawling estate was an architectural marvel and he forced himself to stifle the discomfort at the idea of opening it up to another person, to Maria. But he would. He'd have to. The idea of Maria and his child being anywhere other than with him? Simply untenable.

'You will have access to anything you could want. Truly. But I need you to understand one thing, Maria.' Her eyes grew watchful, assessing, as if she realised that this was the most important thing of all. 'Do not build hopes and fantasies about me. I promise you now, that I will love, care for and provide every single earthly want for our child. But that is the extent of what I will offer.'

He was saying that he wouldn't, couldn't, love her. He was refusing her the one thing she'd only just realised she'd ever wanted. A wave of sorrow crashed over her and she thought, *How funny. An engagement is supposed to be a happy thing.*

She forced herself to focus on what he was offering her. Her child would want for nothing. Her child would grow up with the kind of security she had once taken for granted, until it had been lost. Never would her child experience the shocking devastation she had. Because she would protect their child. She, who had been protected all her life, would become protector and that thought fired her determination more than any other.

'One condition.'

'Anything.' His response, quick and sure.

'It will be a small wedding. No guests.' She didn't want that day to be a public spectacle. Didn't want her family there, her stepmother turning it into a farce. She could already imagine the lascivious glint in Valeria's gaze, the image of her mother in her father's eyes, and the disappointment in her brother's.

'Just us and two witnesses?'

'Yes.'

'It will be so.'

He reached for her hand across the table, the heat of his fingers searing as they wrapped around her cool skin. A handshake, as if nothing more than a contract had been agreed to.

Tears threatened the backs of her eyelids, but she willed them away. Others might be full of joy and brimming with happiness, but she wasn't one of those soon-to-be brides. No. She was a soon-to-be mother and would do whatever it took to care for, protect and love her child in the way that she had not felt herself.

Matthieu might have wanted a quick wedding, but even he, with all his might and money, could not force Swiss bureaucracy to bend to his will. Once their marriage application had passed through the churning machine of legalities and regulations they had still needed to wait ten long days before the ceremony could take place. And Matthieu had used that time well. He might not have known much about Maria before, but, having collected the many required details for the application, he did now.

He was going to be a father.

He almost resented Maria the time she'd had to mentally prepare for impending parenthood. She'd had about a month on him before informing him, but he had been forced to absorb it all in a matter of an hour or two that night. But since then?

The vehemence of the connection he felt to his unborn child shocked him. The determination to protect, to claim, the yearning to meet this heir of his was utterly astounding. So long he had lived, ruthlessly avoiding any sense of commitment or connection to another… He had thought it would chafe, that he would wrangle against it defiantly. But he had been wrong.

As if in a single moment, the compass points of his life had changed, now pointing solely to his child and Maria. And as he looked at himself in the mirror, dark blue suit and a shirt of such pale blue it was almost white, for the first time in more years than he could count he wondered what his father would think. Matthieu searched his own features for traces of the father who had loved him so much he had searched a flame-ridden building to drag Matthieu out, unthinking and unheeding of the danger and damage to himself. Before he had gone back in for his wife.

A blade-sharp pain twisted in his chest before he closed the door on his thoughts.

'Ah, Matthieu.'

He turned to find Malcolm standing in the doorway of his office suite. The older man was nodding in approval. 'They would be so proud of you.'

Matthieu gritted his teeth against the sentiment. He doubted very much that his parents would be proud of his knocking up an innocent and forcing her into a marriage she had no desire for.

'Where is David?' he enquired of Malcolm's husband. The two had finally married once the bill allowing for same-sex marriage had passed in California. After almost eleven years of being together, Malcolm had felt that they didn't really need a piece of paper to certify their relationship, but the battle for legal recognition had been hard fought and hard won, and David and Malcolm had married for the world they wanted as much as the love they already had.

Goosebumps rose over Matthieu's skin, soothed only slightly by the soft cotton of his shirt. He didn't have to wonder if Maria had wanted that kind of love in her life. He knew she had, and for the first time since demanding that she wore his ring, he realised the cost to her, despite having paraded all that she would gain before her.

'David has gone to meet Maria at the hotel. He wanted to walk over to the register office with her.'

Matthieu bit back a curse. How had he not thought of that? Was he truly such a bastard that while he espoused the virtues of what his money could mean to her and their child, he had failed to even see to the first emotional requirement she might have on her wedding day? He would do better. He had to.

Maria stared at herself in the mirror, marvelling that it had almost been easier to pack up her entire life in Camberwell than to find a dress that would suit not only a civil ceremony but the burgeoning baby bump that still caught her by surprise.

Two days ago she had answered the door to an incredibly efficient removal team who had retrieved an almost miserably small stack of boxes containing her clothes, books, the few items of furniture she'd possessed to be sent on to Switzerland. But her equipment—her jewellery, the bits and bobs she'd gathered over the years—had been sent to her brother's estate in Italy. Those boxes must have looked as if they belonged to a very talented magpie: rich colours, sparkling, semi-precious stones, bursting from the seams. Her moulds, her tools and the series of bracelets, rings, earrings and necklaces she had already started to amass had been by far the greatest part of her belongings. For some reason, one she neither could nor would put a finger on, she hadn't wanted to take them to Switzerland.

She had bid a tearful farewell to Evin and Anita, and had allowed herself one last day in the small studio she had rented a space in, up near the Thames in Bermondsey. That was where she'd felt the pull greatest. That was where she had poured her hopes and dreams into the small projects that she had made for her first gallery showing only months earlier. That was where she had returned to after that fateful night with Matthieu and forged a new, determined and optimistic outlook for her future…until she had discovered her pregnancy and all her imaginings had disappeared in a puff of silver smoke.

And now when she thought of her future, one irrevocably bound to the father of her child, her future as his wife, she wondered at it. Would she be expected to be on his arm at business functions, the practically perfect wife? Or would he grow tired of her once she had his child and then package her off to some distant place? She had no idea what his home looked like, where she would be able to find space to create the pieces that were so important to her. Not once in the last two months had she been able to find that heady, almost meditative sense of creativity that would have, in the past, consumed and calmed her.

A knock on the door jolted her from her day dreams. She opened it to a tall, smiling, slightly rotund blond man, who seemed only to smile even more at her evident confusion.

'Maria? I'm David Antoinelli.'

'The witness?' Maria had remembered his name from one of Matthieu's emails.

'Yes,' he laughed easily. 'I did hope that you'd recognise my name. Didn't think you'd appreciate a *complete* stranger knocking on the door the morning of your wedding.'

She pulled the door open wide, gesturing for him to enter.

'I thought you might like someone to walk with you to the register office, given that...' He trailed off, clearly not wanting to point out that she was alone. But his rich, upper-class British accent was so wonderfully familiar, she instantly warmed to him.

'You're English.'

'Ha! Yes. I grew up in North London,' he said, leaning towards her conspiratorially.

'I live—*lived*—in Camberwell.'

'South of the river!' he exclaimed. 'I never really crossed the Thames much, but I did have some rather indecent nights in Vauxhall, but the less said about that to my husband, the better.'

Maria couldn't help the smile that grew on her lips,

and the well of relief that bloomed in her chest. The thought of walking towards her wedding on her own...

'I must say,' he said, taking her in with a beam of approval, 'you look glorious.'

'Thank you,' she said, exhaling a breath of relief. The simple, knee-length dress had an empire waist cinching just above the beginning of her bump and a beautiful sweetheart neckline. The form-fitting cream satin was covered by beautifully detailed lace that rose up the material and covered her arms and décolletage. And even better, she'd been able to afford it with her meagre savings.

She had tamed her curls into braids either side of her head and pinned them up, leaving only a few strands of her dark hair free to frame her face.

David offered her his arm, and she held up a hand for one moment while she gathered the things she would need from the suite. The rest—her small bag of belongings—would, she had been told, be retrieved and sent on to Matthieu's house before they arrived there that evening. She stifled the blush that rose at thoughts of just how that evening would be spent. It was perhaps one of the only things that hadn't yet been negotiated and settled on.

She caught her shawl and the small bouquet of flowers she had ventured out for earlier that morning. She had looked longingly at the sweet bundle of white peonies, sage and rosemary. She knew that a herb bouquet might be slightly unorthodox but she hadn't been able to resist them. With one last glance at herself in the mirror, one last look at herself as a single woman, she bid her adieu, took David's proffered arm and closed the door on her past life, ready to assume the role of Mrs Montcour.

Matthieu and Malcolm were waiting on the steps of the register office he'd deemed perfectly suitable for their needs until he caught sight of Maria. He felt the heated glare of disapproval from Malcolm beside him as his oldest friend looked from Maria and his husband to Matthieu and the building behind him.

Matthieu felt the instant denial on his lips. *I didn't know.* Because he hadn't. He hadn't known she would look so beautiful, almost ethereal. He hadn't expected to see the small, perfectly formed shape of the promise of their child beneath her dress. He hadn't realised that he would see her and think that he had absolutely got it wrong. They should have been in a church—the biggest one he could find, filled with everyone they knew to show off his stunning bride, with pride and adoration shining in his eyes. He just hadn't known that he would feel that way.

When they finally drew close, David pronounced in his usually enthusiastic way, 'If I wasn't an already happily married man, I'd be tempted to run away with the bride.'

'And now that I can see for myself exactly how lovely you are, Maria, I am tempted to do the same,' Malcolm replied, leaning forward to kiss her cheek.

Maria shone beneath the words of their encouragement, and only took a moment to seem slightly bemused at the contrast between his friends' open expressions and his utter silence. Because he was simply incapable of speech. The sight of her had robbed him of it.

The two men embraced leaving Maria and Matthieu to stare at each other, taking in each's appearance in silence, in weighted anticipation of what they were about to do.

'You look…beautiful,' he said, aware that his tone was guttural and hoping that it didn't sound begrudging. Because somewhere deep within, he did feel that way. Strangely resentful that he didn't deserve this. Deserve her. Deserve the child they carried. But Maria most definitely deserved more than he was able and willing to offer.

'Thank you,' she said, casting her eyes away from his as if she was embarrassed or flustered by his simple words.

He guided her into the building, Malcolm and David close behind them as they made their way towards the office where the registrar was waiting for them. Despite the almost ugly functional exterior of the building, the interior was a relief. The rich tones of whisky-coloured wood flooring soothed. Expensive, yet tasteful chairs filled the almost empty room, the focus of which was a beautiful mahogany table where the registrar and the officiant waited to greet them.

Matthieu felt oddly detached from proceedings he'd never thought he'd experience. In every one of his past encounters he'd ensured that the only thing that passed between the women who had shared his bed and himself was pleasure. Given and received—nothing more. Once they had left his life, he gave them little thought. Only that hadn't been true of Maria. There hadn't been an hour that had passed in between that night in Iondorra and the night she'd crashed back into his life with news that had changed everything, that he hadn't thought of her. From the very first moments leaving her bed, he'd tasted her on his tongue, felt her skin beneath his, the echoes of her sighs and gentle laughter, haunting his nights.

Now, he cast a look over to where Maria sat in the corner of the room with the celebrant, presumably going over the same questions that he was currently answering to the registrar. His mind working automatically to supply the requisite information as his heart picked itself up and reached for her.

'Are you ready?'

The question mocked him, but he nodded, swift and sure, knowing what must be done.

She deserved more.

He would give her everything he could, he promised. Not just because of their child. But because she deserved it. She had uprooted her entire life, placed it in his undeserving hands and no matter what the future brought them, he would make sure that she was protected.

'We are gathered here today…'

Maria let the words wash over her. She had wondered how she'd feel, ever since agreeing to Matthieu's outrageous proclamation that they would marry, and now that she was here, now that she stood before the registrar and officiant and they were saying the words that every young girl had dreamed of hearing as a child, she just didn't know. She didn't know how she felt. She had expected fear, but—she thought, resisting the urge to shake her head—that wasn't what she felt. Defiance? No, not that either. Hesitation? Oddly, no. Not even that. Numb, she decided. Numb as the words brought her closer and closer to the moment she would be bound to Matthieu for ever.

She suddenly felt as if she'd left something behind. That she'd forgotten something vital, but couldn't for the life of her think what it was. She frowned, then realised that the officiant had said something that required a response from her. Mistaking her lack of response for nerves, the officiant smiled and repeated the question.

'Will you, Maria, take Matthieu to be your lawful wedded husband?'

No words of love in this perfunctory service, then. No honouring above all else. But she wasn't doing this for herself. She was doing this for their child. There would be love, would be honouring above all else. There would be protection and security and…

'I will.'

'And will you, Matthieu, take Maria to be your lawful wedded wife?'

Finally Maria found the courage to look to Matthieu then, startled somewhat to find him gazing at her with an intensity that reminded her immediately of that night. In his eyes she saw the lake in Iondorra, she saw the stars that blanketed the night sky. She saw the deep pull of arousal in his eyes, hypnotic and unfathomable. And if her heart hurt, because for just a moment she saw how it could have been, she chided herself for wanting more.

'I will.'

'The rings?'

Rings. That was what she'd forgotten. She didn't know a single jewellery maker who hadn't spent hours pouring attention and passion into a creation that symbolised a couple's love for each other. She had once thought that she might make her own and her future husband's. There was a special part of her designs and sketches that, long ago, she'd thought she might use as the basis for what she would one day wear for the rest of her life. But the intensity of the last few weeks, the practicalities, had thrown that from her mind. And for a moment she was relieved. Because this was not what she'd wanted. Not really. While Matthieu reached to his pocket, she ran a hand over the lower part of her abdomen. The small, firm bump cradling her soon-to-be child.

She realised that Matthieu's eyes had snagged on the movement, and hesitated just a second before he produced something from his pocket. He reached for her hand and held the ring in his fingers in such a way that she couldn't see it until he had slipped it over her finger.

And she stared.

Stared and stared. Because in some impossible way it was perfect. As if he'd found what she wanted without her even knowing it. The silver band gave way to a circle of small diamonds encasing a beautifully cut shard of jet.

'This is how I see us, Maria,' he whispered to her. 'Joined together, surrounding our child with love and security, with protection.'

The sincerity and certainty shining in his eyes settled about her, her heart aching with the want of love, but appeased by the promise he was offering her. Not of fairy tales of happy-ever-afters, not with offers of obscene wealth that meant nothing to her, not with lies of unfelt emotions, but a promise of everything he could and would do for her and her child. Their child.

'I now declare you husband and wife.'

CHAPTER FIVE

MARIA BREATHED IN the cool scents of water and woods. She had been walking for twenty minutes towards Lake Lucerne, marvelling once again at the sheer breadth of acreage within Matthieu's estate.

She shook her head at the beauty of the sight before her. Water spreading out like a spool of molten silver, reflecting the blue of the cloudless sky and the stunning emerald greens of the trees bordering the banks of the lake.

Her fingers rubbed against each other, soothing the nipping bite of the cold against her skin, brushing gently the band of silver, diamond and jet that she had worn now for almost a month. Nothing had been as she'd imagined. Nothing she'd expected or dreamed of that moment he had slipped the ring over her finger had come to pass.

After their wedding ceremony, David and Malcolm and whisked them away to one of Bern's most renowned restaurants for an exquisite wedding breakfast, nothing of which she remembered tasting. If the jovial couple had noticed anything peculiar in the silence between the newly minted husband and wife, neither acknowledged it. Their happy, gentle, mocking banter had washed over her before the limousine had arrived to take her and Matthieu to his home, here on the edge of Lake Lucerne.

She remembered sitting beside Matthieu in the dark cocoon of the luxurious interior of the sleek machine that ferried them towards their wedding night, tension palpable and thrumming from where he held himself almost impossibly still and she practically vibrated with it. In clipped words he had told her about his home, the team of staff employed to service, clean and cook for them, the extensive gym and leisure equipment, including an infinity pool that overlooked Switzerland's famous lake. The walks that had been cleared throughout the estate, the woodlands and down to the shorefront.

'Anything is yours,' he'd said.

Apart from you, she'd noted silently.

As the limousine had eaten up the miles of smooth tarmac, winding closer and closer towards their destination, she had wondered why on earth he was talking. Reams of descriptions about the house, the architect, the way life would be, and all she could think was, *Yes, but what about now? What about tonight?* Because in truth she had been almost overcome by a maddening sense of him. Everything about the previous weeks had been about practicalities, packing up her home and life, getting to the register office, the exchanging of rings and signing of marriage certificates… But the moment it had happened, the moment that they had been declared husband and wife—she blushed now at the memory of it—all she had thought of was spending the night with her husband.

She had wanted to share his bed, to feel even just for a little the same kind of 'rightness' she had experienced the night they had conceived their child. To feel the heady sense of desire, the way that their bodies had somehow communicated beyond words or civilities but more with raw, intense and all-consuming passion. An equal passion—the one thing that they had most definitely shared.

It hadn't gone away, she'd marvelled as they'd drawn closer and closer to Matthieu's estate. She had seen her husband in the sweep of the passing road lights, illuminating the darkness that surrounded their journey. The soft dark swirls of his beard doing little to gentle the stark outline of his jaw. The thick dark brows almost startling atop eyes of pure molten honey that gleamed almost with traces of emerald. The width and breadth of him made her feel deliciously small, delicate but also strong—strong in her desire for him, the need to make that physical contact, any kind of contact with the man she had just married.

And when they had finally drawn to a halt at the top of a sweeping driveway beyond a set of stunning iron electronically controlled gates, she had thought, *This is it*. She had turned to him, just in front of the large wooden door to a building she had been unable to take in because of the sheer magnificence of her husband, her hand poised to raise to his jaw, her palms itching to feel the heat of him, the soft whorl of his beard against her skin, just as he'd pushed open the door, explained where her room was and stalked off to his 'office'.

He had left her standing in the foyer of an unknown home, alone, in her wedding dress, untouched and unwanted.

She had retreated to the room he had given some offhand directions to before the first tear had fallen. She had kicked off her shoes, before the second and third, she had collapsed onto the bed and pressed her face into the pillow before the sounds of her sobs could be heard. Because it was then that she'd realised what she had done. She had looked for love for her entire life and now she had consigned herself to a man who would never love her.

As she turned her back on the beautiful lake and made her way back to the estate, Maria realised she had neither of the futures she'd envisioned for herself just before the wedding. She was not his perfect wife, nor the discarded wife. Instead, he had put her in this strange kind of half-life, and she feared that it was slowly choking her.

No matter what he did, Matthieu couldn't shake the stranglehold that had wrapped around his chest. Couldn't escape the realisation, sheer and shocking, that he had done something very wrong. It had started that first night they had come here. Before that even, in the limousine bringing them home. *Home*. He'd not really ever thought of this place as a home before. It was his sanctuary, yes, the place he hid away from the outside world. But a home?

In the limousine, he'd felt it. The sensual undercurrent ebbing and flowing between them. As it had done that first night in Iondorra, her expressive features, her body, it had called to him. Teased and tempted him. The thick band of arousal fierce and shocking, as everything in him roared to reach out and take what he wanted, to take *her*.

But he had meant the promise he'd made to himself, to Maria silently, the day of their wedding. He meant to protect her. Which meant that he needed to ensure that they started their marriage as it would continue. He would give her her every material need or desire. But he could not give her himself. Because if he lifted the tight leash he had on his control, if he did what he so desperately wanted, to sink into her soft warm heat, to give into the exquisite pleasure that she brought him, he wouldn't be able to hold himself back. And he couldn't shake the thought that doing so would unleash the thoughts and memories he felt biting at the edges of his consciousness.

So he *had* held himself back from her that night and all the nights since. And if that meant he had to suffer this constant state of frustration, then so be it.

His legs pounded away on the treadmill of the sprawling gym housed on the floor beneath the living quarters and kitchen, and two floors beneath the bedrooms and infinity pool that stretched out towards the lake.

Sweat dripped down the sides of his head and he swiped at it with his arm. If he could exhaust himself, perhaps then he would find relief from this...thing. This feeling in him that felt like a ragged beast, tearing and snarling away in his chest.

Exercise had become something vital for him over the years. It had started with the rehabilitation after hours, days, weeks of surgeries in the years following the fire. He barely remembered those first few months. A pain so intense it had made him delirious with agony, which at times he'd actually been thankful for. Because it focused his mind on something other than the fact he had lost his entire family. Something other than the last look his father gave him, having hurled him from the living-room window before turning back for his mother.

His feet and legs compensated for the shiver that ran through his body, the heat and sweat turning icy cold beneath the memory of the screams from that night. Their screams, his screams, he couldn't tell. But neither his mother, his father, nor his uncles and aunt had escaped the inferno that had consumed the old estate.

Faulty electrics, a real Christmas tree, and a two-hundred-year-old estate. That was what the insurance investigation had decreed. An accident. An accident that had robbed him of everything.

He increased the treadmill's speed in an attempt to force his focus to shift back to nothing more than the movement of his feet and body. He never dwelled on thoughts of his family. He had become adept at avoiding them but as he picked up the pace, to run almost flat out, he couldn't shake the feeling that perhaps he was running from his past.

Because unaccountably since Maria had moved into his home, he'd felt it rising up around him. Memories of family meals, the echoes of childhood laughter at his parents' gentle mocking, or the warm love they offered, they all hovered around Maria like a promise of what could be, but what he would not allow himself.

So Matthieu had begun to avoid her, plunging himself into work, into new acquisitions. He'd even left her here while he'd travelled to one of the mines in Russia, hoping that the distance between them would cause things to settle back into what his life had been like before. But the moment he'd returned, he'd seen signs of her throughout the estate. Books left on side tables, a throw on the sofa that hadn't been there before. Having lived alone for more than ten years, he'd found it disconcerting. It had felt like an intrusion and, although he shouldn't, he found himself begrudging her for it. For presenting reminders, evidence of what she had done without him.

And soon it wouldn't just be evidence of his wife…it would be their child. Would he spend his future trying to avoid them both? *No*, he growled internally. Once again shocked by the possessiveness of his feelings towards his child.

A noise startled him and he nearly lost his footing.

His hands flew to the bar in front of him to steady himself, as he mentally checked the ankle he'd nearly turned over, cursing loudly.

'Sorry! I didn't...'

'It's okay,' he said, between huge lungfuls of air, not having to look up again to know what had caused him to nearly fall from the speeding mill beneath him. He reached out and decreased the speed, waiting until it had slowed to a walk before casting a look up at the doorway.

He was already breathing hard when he took in the sight of her, thankful that he had a reason to disguise his body's natural reaction to her beauty, to her presence. She was simply glorious.

The long dark loose curls fell over her bare shoulders and hovered near her waist. Her leggings clung to shapely legs and he had a sudden and shocking urge to wrap his palm around the curve of her thigh. He drenched himself in memories of that night for just a moment before flinging the door closed on that train of thought. He was still staring at the way the vest clung to her breasts and to where it pulled tight across the increasing swell around her stomach. No. It was no longer a swell and had—in the last few weeks—most definitely formed into a bump. He marvelled at how her body had changed even in the weeks since their wedding, and couldn't help the word forming in his mind possessively and with no uncertain amount of finality...*mine*.

* * *

Maria had heard him curse and was startled that it echoed the exact same thought crashing through her mind. She hadn't expected to find him here having returned from her walk by the lake, convinced that he had left before dawn to head to his office, as he had done almost every single day since their wedding.

But he was here. And he looked...

Her mouth actually watered.

Seriously, she thought to herself, *am I that base?*

Yes. Yes, I most definitely am.

A pair of soft grey sweatpants hung low on lean hips, showing off the taut muscles dipping beneath its waistband. Because, naturally, he was shirtless, and all-consumingly magnificent. The breadth of his arms, the sheen of sweat covering his skin, her eyes ate up every inch of him. The scars becoming less something that she noted, but more something that highlighted the way his sculpted muscles shifted along with his body's movements.

She regretted the moment he reached for the T-shirt hanging from the bars of the treadmill, almost begged him not to cover up such sheer masculine beauty, and she very much hated that he felt he had to cover his body for her. He pulled it over his head, tugging it down over the breadth of his chest, and cut off the sight that had both shocked and enticed.

'I wanted to do some yoga and thought that...' She felt that she had to fill the silence, otherwise they might just continue to stare at each other, like combatants facing off against…what? Their desires? Their wants? Because she knew that he wanted her. She could see it in his eyes. And that made his almost continual absence from her presence so much harder to bear. She cut off thoughts that were beginning to feel a little too self-pitying and made her way over to the soft mat flooring by the floor-to-ceiling mirrors.

'Of course,' he said as he started to leave.

'I…' she started, and then stopped, as he looked confused as to why she might want to continue to talk to him. Might want him here. She cursed inwardly again. She couldn't go on like this. She couldn't live like this. Two separate people in one house, barely seeing or speaking to each other. 'I thought I'd take the car into town this morning.'

'You have an obstetrician appointment?' he asked, surprised, as if scanning his memory for some piece of missing information.

'No,' Maria replied, shaking her head, her curls cascading down the bare skin on her shoulders and back. That had been one of the last things they'd done together, met with the obstetrician—an efficient, kind Swiss national with gleaming offices and state-of-the-art equipment. They weren't due to visit Ms Klein for another three weeks. 'I wanted to go shopping.'

'What for?'

'A dress for the gala.'

'What gala?'

She shivered at his tone, which was cut through with shards of icicles. She frowned, wondering whether it was the purchase of the dress that bothered him or the attendance at the gala they'd received an invitation to.

It had been the first and only piece of correspondence sent to her—well, *them*—since her arrival at Matthieu's estate and the gentle scrolling swirl, *Mr and Mrs Montcour*, had caught her eye. She had been faintly surprised that she was acknowledged as his wife, not thinking that the news of their marriage had become public knowledge yet, but then had seen the silver insignia of Montcour Mining Industries in the bottom right-hand corner of the embossed invitation. Perhaps he had meant to tell her about the gala, presuming her to have a spare ball gown that would fit a burgeoning baby bump hanging in her closet. Either way, it didn't matter. She *was* Mrs Montcour and as such had absolutely every right to open a letter addressed to her.

'The one in Lausanne, this evening,' she said slowly and clearly, because surely he was feigning such a blank, strange reaction. 'I must say, I was a little surprised to find that you have a charity.'

'I have three goldmines, two diamond mines and a multibillion-dollar business, why would it surprise you that I have a charity?'

'Please don't tell me it's just a tax write-off,' she bit back, resenting the dismissive list of his impressive assets. And suddenly she was angry. Angry that he seemed to think that she wouldn't want to attend a charity gala they had been invited to. Angry that he insisted on leaving her alone to roam this sprawling, yet luxurious estate. A place seemingly made entirely of concrete and steel, the cold greys serving only to remind her constantly of its aloof owner. Angry that she felt she had had to explain or justify her movements. Surely she wasn't trapped here and could come and go as she pleased?

'We won't be going,' he said, his tone almost a growl and his hand cutting through the air between them as if punctuating his decree.

'Why not?'

'I have business to attend to.'

'Well, I don't.' The thought of spending yet another night alone suddenly became impossible to her and everything in her wanted to escape. He looked at her then as if her wants and needs didn't matter. As if she had grown two heads and four extra arms and he simply couldn't understand her desire for more.

Enough. She'd had enough of tiptoeing around the father of her child.

'So I will be going,' she said, staring up at the stone effigy that her husband had become. 'You, however, don't have to. In fact, I'd rather you didn't. Because I find that I don't want you to spoil this evening for me, in the same way that you have spoiled almost every day since our wedding,' she said on a shaky breath, drawing strength from her new determination. 'I refuse to live like this, Matthieu. Yes, you might have offered me every material comfort within our marriage, but a person, a *human being*, cannot live in isolation and it's driving me crazy. I don't think that I've actually had a longer conversation with anyone beyond, "Hi, how are you?" "Fine, thanks, and you?" in over three and a half weeks! I know more about Tomas, your driver, than I do about you. He has three children, by the way—not sure if you know that—and he likes his coffee with a hint of caramel, though he doesn't like his wife to know as she's been after him to watch his calorie intake. Matthieu, tell me, how do you like your coffee?'

It was as if the dam had broken within her against the almost unending silence of the last few weeks and words—nonsensical words—had flowed forth like a flood. She was almost breathless from the speed with which she'd delivered her little speech, and now she held her breath, waiting to see how Matthieu would respond.

'How I like my coffee is irrelevant, Maria. We, you, I, or any combination thereof, will *not* be going to the gala. If you want to go out, Tomas will take you anywhere you wish to go. But only if that somewhere has the very limited possibility of your outing being uncovered by the press. And as that will not be the case of the gala this evening, you will not be attending.'

She shouldn't have been surprised. He stalked from the room without a word and she felt even more furious than she had before. Press or no, she would not be a prisoner here any longer.

Maria sat in the back of the limousine, the partition down between her and Tomas, who had kept a gentle running commentary since leaving Matthieu's estate in Lucerne, and she was thankful because if he hadn't the two-and-a-half-hour drive would have given Maria too much time to think. To wonder at what she was doing and how Matthieu would react when he realised she had defied his decree and sneaked out of his estate like a runaway child. This was the first time that she would have crossed him. But he didn't understand. She had needed to. She needed *this*.

Mrs Montcour.

Was she? Really? Given they hadn't consummated the marriage. Did something like consummation work retrospectively? And even if it did, who was this strange Mrs Montcour? Maria had been many things, the daughter of an exiled Duke, the sister of an international playboy, an art student, coffee-shop worker, jewellery maker. But now she was a wife, and would be a mother. And somewhere swirling amongst the discomfort in her belly was the fear that she didn't know how to be this person.

She had considered reaching out to her brother, but Sebastian had been unusually preoccupied recently, simply accepting her explanation that she had gone to stay with a friend in Switzerland for 'a while', rather than interrogating her over every minute detail as he usually did. As for her father, well, months could go by without speaking to him and she couldn't help but hide behind the familiar feeling that it was easier for her father not to see her and be reminded so painfully of his dead wife.

She had thought of reaching out to Anita and Evin, but what would she say? I tracked down the father of my child, happens to be a billionaire several times over, we married for the sake of the child and he whisked me off to his secluded lair?

The only person she had to tether her to her new role was Matthieu and he seemed hell-bent on leaving her alone and untouched.

'We're here, Mrs Montcour,' Tomas said, in his crisp Swiss-French accent.

It was then that she realised she hadn't really thought this through. She hadn't expected a red carpet, even pre-warned, she hadn't expected the sprawling mass of paparazzi lining the street to the entrance of the grand building where the gala was being held.

Maria stepped out of the limousine on autopilot. What had she been thinking? Would they even know who she was? Or would they think her some impostor trying to sneak into the gala? As far as she knew, no one had identified her, no one knew her as Mrs Montcour. She cursed as she drew to a halt, staring somewhat in horror at the huge sprawling mass of reporters and photographers quite possibly about to witness the ultimate humiliation of her being refused entry.

Tomas closed the door behind her and stood beside her as if ready to reopen the door and shove her unceremoniously back into the sleek black machine. Until a small, suited man holding a clipboard rushed up to meet her.

'Welcome…'

The query in his voice was so clear that it echoed within her chest. All her fears, all her questions, it was now down to her to own this new person she had come to be, whatever the consequence.

'Mrs Montcour,' she replied, hiding behind a steady voice.

The look on the man's face would have been comical under any other circumstances and she couldn't help the feeling that perhaps he wasn't going to believe her. Her fingers gripped the embossed invitation ready to thrust it towards him as if in evidence of her claim.

'Of course,' he said, shaking his head as if she might disappear at any moment. 'It is…*wonderful* to meet you. We had not expected your attendance this evening, given that…' Whatever he might have been about to say was cut short as he stepped back slightly, his gaze drawn to the bump positioned almost between them. 'May I offer my congratulations, Mrs Montcour?' The pure beam of happiness shining from this small, suited stranger was oddly infectious, and she couldn't help but sweep a hand over her unborn child.

'Thank you,' she said, smiling, as the first flash of the bulb cut through their conversation, nearly blinding her. It was then that the shouts started and starburst-like strobe lighting covered her from head to toe. She vaguely saw the man gesture for her to follow him and, keeping her gaze down on the red carpet and away from the bright lights, she made her way into the gala, her heart pounding and irrationally slightly afraid.

Once up the stairs and through the grand entrance to the museum that had been co-opted for the gala, Maria blew out a shaky breath.

'My apologies for the scrum, Mrs Montcour, it is a necessary evil, but the notoriety brings much attention and finances for our charity.' The seemingly endless stream of dialogue coming from the small man was as much of a shock as the press had been. And suddenly Maria wasn't sure that she wanted to be here. Couldn't help herself longing for the quiet peaceful solitude of Matthieu's estate.

'Mr Montcour regrettably has been unable to attend our events in Lausanne for many years, the invitation is usually sent out as a courtesy, but we are truly honoured that you have come.' Maria found nothing but sincerity in the man's words, soothing some of her initial reluctance.

'That's very kind of you to say...'

'Benjamin Keant,' he supplied.

'Benjamin. It is lovely to meet you.'

'Charmed, Mrs Montcour. Simply charmed. Would you allow me to introduce you to some of the other patrons and guests? I can also tell you anything you'd like to know about our charity.'

Maria smiled, thankful that she could disguise her ignorance. 'Absolutely. And why don't you imagine that I know absolutely nothing about your charity and start from the very beginning?'

Already she had realised that she'd drawn the curious gazes of the many guests she could see in the large open foyer of the museum. It distracted her from the start of Benjamin's spiel, until she caught words that fired an alarm instantly within her mind and heart.

'And the money raised here is put back not only into the medical centres that deal with such devastating burn injuries, but rehabilitation, financial support for families who may struggle with the exorbitant costs of years-long, if not life-long, medical care, and emotional counselling and support for all affected.'

Burn injuries. Medical care. Emotional counselling.

A cold shiver passed over Maria's shoulder blades and down her spine as she realised exactly why Matthieu might not have wanted to be here. It had nothing to do with her whatsoever, and everything to do with him and what had happened to him all those years ago.

CHAPTER SIX

LONG BEFORE THE whirring blades of the helicopter slowed after touching down on the discreet helipad in the back of the museum's gardens, Matthieu's jaw had clenched in a vice-like grip. It had nothing to do with the hastily rescheduled phone meeting with the South African Ambassador about future mining prospects and everything to do with his runaway wife. He forced himself to loosen his jaw or risk losing a molar. Instead the tension travelled to his hands as he took long, powerful strides across the manicured pathways towards the gala, fisting and un-fisting fingers that topped white knuckles.

He did *not* want to be here. In fact, he had not attended the charity in nearly ten years, ever since that first time. Memories coursed through his veins, thickening the blood with anger and frustration, and something a little like scorn at his naivety back then. He'd had such great hopes of what the charity would become, but from the very first moment, the very first flash of a paparazzo's camera he'd realised that the vultures had descended not to support the charity but to feast on the wounds left by the loss of his family. To feast upon him. All of the resulting photographs and press had been so focused on the notorious Matthieu Montcour, with all but a few lines about the legacy he'd wanted to create. That night he'd sworn never to attend again, never to detract from the charity, to taint it with his own burgeoning reputation as a beast. Instead he had left the running of the charity to the highly efficient man he had appointed almost ten years ago. Not for a second did he regret founding the charity—he just couldn't have anything to do with it personally.

But Maria had no idea what she was walking into. The press, the celebrities who attended his event feasted on gossip and drama as much as water to live and breathe, and the discovery that he had not only married but had impregnated his wife would be irresistible fodder for tomorrow's headlines.

On the short flight over he had already fired off an email to his secretary to handle the impending fallout of the news. Security would be tightened not only at his office, but at each of his properties, including the estate in Lucerne. He hated living under a microscope, having done so both medically and publicly ever since the deaths of his parents.

What did you think? an inner voice chided. *That you could keep Maria to yourself? That you could keep her and your child a secret for ever? Keep Maria to yourself?*

The words ran through his mind, almost like a directive, an order, a demand.

I refuse to live like this.

Maria's words from earlier that day in the gym had cut through him like a knife and he cursed, wondering for a moment if he had truly become a monster, locking her away in his home, keeping her isolated from the rest of the world.

But she didn't understand. She didn't know what it was like.

Two black suited men stood either side of the small white entrance to the back of the building, swirling white wires betraying the discreet earpieces indicating their business here. Noting his arrival, they cast an assessing gaze over him, almost in unison, their faces utterly impassive, before one pushed open the door allowing Matthieu entrance to the museum.

A small, blonde woman met him on the other side, simple make-up adding a professional sheen to her face in the absence of a smile. That was what he'd liked about Margery, the charity director's assistant. Unlike most, she didn't fawn, paw or even, like now, smile. Crisp, unemotional efficiency. The kind he'd always surrounded himself with…until Maria.

Margery explained in her no-nonsense way that Maria had arrived thirty minutes earlier, had been met by the charity's director, Mr Keant—never Benjamin, she never used his first name—but that the press had almost been rabid at the realisation of her identity. Keant had ushered his wife down the red carpet unharmed and was now introducing her to various guests. The keynote speech would start in five minutes, the dinner in thirty, and the quickest possible exit he could make without drawing undue attention would be after the dinner, which would conclude in ninety minutes.

He nodded as they came to another discreet door, accepting the information, digesting it, before he swiftly stepped through the door into the large foyer of the museum where the main reception was being held.

He saw her immediately, halting mid-stride at the sight of her. She was stunning. The midnight-blue dress had been drenched in a million tiny sequins, the material clinging to every curve, every inch of the perfect bump riding low on her abdomen, down over her thighs and reaching all the way to a pair of high heels that sparkled silver glints in the spot lighting high above them on the museum's domed interior. *Mine.* Everything in him roared with satisfaction, as if he'd found the one and only thing he'd wanted since he'd left the gym and retreated to his office earlier in the day, not even once imagining that she would defy him.

She was speaking to a couple, the woman holding a young baby, and the man holding the hand of a boy of about seven. She was laughing. That was what had struck him still. He hadn't seen her laugh since that night in Iondorra. Her hand was outstretched in front of her, where the baby was gripping her silver bangles and tugging on them, bringing more laughter from her peach-coloured lips.

His gaze searched the tableau, finally resting on the young boy, whose smile wasn't dimmed in the slightest by the slash of scar tissue reaching up from his neck and covering half of the child's face. There was no way for the boy to hide the damaged skin, not as Matthieu could.

He felt a sharp stab of pain in his chest, shocking and powerful as he took in the sight. All around him were patrons and guests of his charity, all ready and more than willing to donate to a more than worthy cause. And yes, there were a few glances his way, but most of the attendees were wrapped up in their present conversations. Here were people who had been affected, just like him, those who had fared both better and far worse than he.

Something harsh skittered over his skin, sending a shiver down his spine. All this time he had stayed away, telling himself that he hadn't wanted to take away attention from the charity, but for the first time, he wondered whether that was the true reason he had avoided the charity for so many years. Because the people who were here, the people who bore similar scars to him, rather than hiding away, stood proudly beneath the lights of the museum, bared themselves to the world and still smiled, still laughed.

In that moment, as if she had sensed his presence, Maria caught his gaze and a whole raft of emotions cried out loud and clear across the crowded room. Surprise, concern, apology and compassion. And all he wanted to see was flaming desire. The same sensation burning deep within him. He pushed away the sudden and shocking arousal, and stalked towards her in firm, quick strides.

'Matthieu…' she said, her voice slightly breathless. 'You came.'

'I did,' he managed to bite out beneath the swirls of resentment and shocking half-thought-out self-revelations.

'Thank you,' she replied, with a smile that soothed, and in that moment he caught just a glimpse of what kind of mother she would become. He'd told her that night at his office that she would be strong, defiant and determined. But now he could see that she would be kind, loving, supportive…all the things his own mother had been.

Suddenly he was plunged back into a memory—one from early in the evening of the fire. His mother was helping him with his tie for the meal they would share with their family. *You look so handsome. Just like your father.* She'd swept him up in an embrace that was tight—one he'd squirmed within—but was full of love and something a little like hope for what he would become. She'd kissed him on his forehead and taken his hand…

'Mr Montcour!' Benjamin Keant practically squealed, having discovered his arrival. 'It is so good to see you here.'

Matthieu shook off the shocking effect of a memory he had not delved into once since the night of the accident, simultaneously yearning for and strangely resenting the remembered feeling of his mother's embrace.

He ignored the varied ramblings of the director, but he couldn't shake the overly watchful gaze of his wife—the wife that saw far too much.

Maria had felt the pull from Matthieu almost as more of a physical tug than the hold the lovely little baby currently had on her bracelets. She had been talking to the couple and their children, finding relief in their easy open conversation more than the vacuous twitterings of the famous socialites or patrons attending the charity gala. Forging even more of a yearning to hold her own child one day.

But then she'd felt it. His gaze lifting the light hair on her arms, a tingling at the back of her neck. When she'd finally seen him, stalking towards her through the crowd, her breath had caught at the sight of him. Impossibly broad shoulders encased in a midnight-blue tux, the material pulled tight across the muscles on his arms, his dark tie pulled slightly at the neck of a startling white shirt as if he'd yanked at it in frustration. On many it would have looked disrespectful. On Matthieu it looked irresistible.

His dark brow and beard accentuated the severe look on features that softened momentarily when he took in the sight of her standing with the young family whose son, Edward, had been caught in a car accident that had swiftly turned life-threatening when the petrol tank had leaked and gone up in flames.

Though the charity director had released an almost

unstoppable flow of words at her husband, apparently failing to discern the dark mood swirling about him, Matthieu had not once taken his eyes from her. She felt it almost as a physical touch, a caress, a brand across her skin. A promise of something she couldn't quite identify and once again she felt herself hurtling towards some kind of impending confrontation and welcomed it. She'd meant what she'd said to him earlier. She couldn't, *wouldn't*, live like this.

'I like your bracelets,' Edward said, reaching up to where his baby sister was still shaking them to produce a tinkling she took great joy in.

'Thank you, Edward,' Maria replied, unable to keep the beam of pride from her voice. 'I made them myself, so the fact you like them makes it extra special for me.'

'You make jewellery?' he asked. She thought of the boxes she had sent to Italy, initially unsure how to work her past into this new present—her marriage. But over the last weeks she had filled sketch pad upon sketch pad, ideas brimming from the stunning surroundings of the estate by Lake Lucerne. The beautiful natural structures of the woods, the trees, leaves and berries… The smooth, mirror-like surface of the water, the reflections to be found there, working with the solitude to fire her imagination. It had been strange to suddenly find this creativity—one that had been languishing, despite her faith and belief in her work, ever since she had left Iondorra. Ever since she had left his bed that first and only time.

'I do,' she decided, realising that it was as much part of her as the baby growing within her.

'And what will you do when you grow up?' Matthieu asked, a tone to his voice Maria didn't think she'd heard before.

Edward peered up at him, cast a quick glance to his parents as if to ask if it would be okay to speak to the stranger and, receiving encouraging smiles, answered, 'I am going to be a firefighter,' with no small amount of pride and determination.

'That would be a very exciting job—and a very important one too.'

'I know,' Edward said, almost dismissively, in that easy childlike way, of his scars.

Matthieu crouched down, bringing his huge frame to Edward's level. 'I do too,' he whispered conspiratorially, lifting back the shirt collar as he had once done with her. Maria held her breath as Edward's eyes grew wide and round, then narrowed in assessment. 'I had skin taken from my head and used in the graft on my face.'

'Wow,' Matthieu said, letting out a low whistle of awe that seemed to satisfy Edward greatly. 'Okay,' he said, making it clear that he was giving something deep consideration and bringing a surprising smile to Maria's lips. '*I* had *fake* skin used in my graft.'

'Split or full thickness?' Edward fired back challengingly.

Maria's skin vibrated with the rumble of laughter let loose by Matthieu and she couldn't help but feel it within her too as she watched her husband and the young boy compare and compete over their various conditions and treatments, seeing for the first time how he might be with their child. The bond she wanted and yearned for between them. 'Are you sure you don't want to be a doctor when you grow up, rather than a fireman?' Matthieu asked.

'I like the fire truck best.'

The group's responding laughter was cut short by the gala's welcoming speech. Benjamin spoke clearly, and surprisingly slowly, on how the money raised would be put to use, and introduced a few of the inspiring success stories from some of the guests present, leaving barely a dry eye in the room, before turning his final thanks and debts of gratitude to Matthieu himself.

Maria shivered from the effect of hundreds of pairs of eyes on her and the powerful man beside her, who managed to hide the discomfort she imagined he must be feeling as he gracefully accepted the acknowledgement and thanks of the charity director. As the cheers from the crowd died down, and Edward and his family disappeared into the throng, Maria finally turned to her husband.

'Do you regret coming tonight?' she asked tentatively. She watched him choose his response carefully.

'Not yet, but the night is still young,' the ironic tone to his voice a fragile olive branch.

She smiled up at him then, reaching for his hand, slipping her fingers in between his, and marvelled at the jolt of electricity and happiness that shot through her as he squeezed gently, the light pressure saying so much more than his brief, carefully chosen words.

As Matthieu took her hand in his he looked about and saw the good that had been done by the charity he'd created from his family's insurance pay-outs. The help it had brought others. Both his uncles and his aunt had been younger than his parents with no children of their own and, as Matthieu was their next of kin, their wealth had all been funnelled his way. More money than he could ever imagine spending in a hundred lifetimes. On top of Montcour Mining Industries it would have seemed almost laughable, if it had not been tied to such a great loss.

Ever since that first gala almost ten years before, the intrusive press, the headlines of the 'haunted Montcour' taking precedence, he had vowed not to return. But in doing so, had he shut himself off from what the charity had achieved? Seeing the hundreds of people, if not more, that the charity was helping…it was as if his family had reached out to so many people in need and worked to help them when and however they needed it. It soothed an ache he'd thought buried too deep to reach.

He was about to turn to Maria when Margery appeared at their side.

'There is still a little time before dinner and Mr Keant thought you might like to see a private viewing of the exhibition the museum has put on display for the gala? They have been incredibly generous with their chosen pieces.'

'Can we?' Maria asked, hopefully. The excitement in her eyes shone as purely as ever and he couldn't refuse her in this.

'Lead the way,' he said, gesturing to Margery.

Once they were through the throng of guests, the quiet of the hallways felt oddly deafening, punctuated by the tapping of his companions' heels on the smooth stone flooring. Through dimly lit corridors they made their way towards a series of rooms closed off for the gala's exhibition.

'If you have any questions about the artists, please don't hesitate to ask,' Margery stated before unclipping the thick red twist of rope across the entrance to the first room. She hung back as Matthieu and Maria made their way into the surprisingly large space.

White walls gave way to incredible splashes of colour as the large paintings hung strategically on the walls led the viewer through and around the space, not chronologically or by subject matter from what he could tell, but more by shape or colour.

The quiet settled a kind of peace about them that washed over him, easing away what suddenly felt like years of tension. Maria walked between the paintings, searching for something he couldn't quite identify. He smiled, realising that she didn't waste time hanging back with undue reverence afforded to an artist based solely on fame, but instead drew up close to certain canvasses as if trying to work out how, rather than why, it was done.

While she studied the paintings, he seemed incapable of not studying her. Her reaction, delight, the slight scrunch of her nose when she found something distasteful, the way her eyes and body lit up with joy when she discovered a masterpiece she'd never thought to see in person. He marvelled again, not only at her beauty, but at his own ability to stay away from her these last few weeks.

They moved from room to room, Margery hanging back discreetly giving them a false feeling of isolation. But Matthieu rarely took his eyes from Maria, which was why it took him a moment to see it for himself. The painting. The one he'd never seen until now.

Maria was almost overwhelmed by the sheer beauty of the collection curated by the museum for the charity gala. Monet, Klee, Caillebotte, Duchamp, Renoir, Rothko, Freud—it was as if they'd gathered the greatest artists of the last two centuries. Everything from rural scenes, portraits, to sculpture and her eyes, heart and mind feasted on it. She felt overwhelmed by the beauty of these pieces, inspired to draw, to delve into her moulds, to melt down the materials to their base states and morph them into something even half as beautiful as what currently surrounded her.

They had come to the last room in the small, but exquisite exhibition and, although there was a huge Hockney taking up almost the entire length of one wall, she couldn't help but be drawn to a much smaller canvas, which depicted a couple and a young boy, all facing each other and laughing together. It wasn't the usual stiff, formal portrait, like others she had passed in the previous rooms. This was the kind that made you smile instantly, the artist somehow managing to include the viewer in a private joke, whilst also making them a voyeur to a family so engrossed in each other they were unaware of being watched. She frowned a little at the father, something about him snagged in her mind, and her gaze flicked to the small white placard, taking in the name of the artist and the family.

She felt as if she had been drenched in water from an ice bucket and couldn't have prevented her gasp of shock if she'd tried. Her hand flew to her mouth, trying a little too late to bring it back as her eyes flew back to take in the details of Matthieu's mother and father... and the young boy he had once been.

A wave of overwhelming sadness and grief covered her as she marvelled at the way the artist had managed to capture the love shining from Matthieu's father's eyes as he gazed at his wife and child. The way his mother only had eyes for young Matthieu, but still had her hand on his father's arm as if their connection was and would always be inviolate. But it was the joy that rocked her. The joy they had in each other...a joy that would be cut short within a year of the painting.

For a moment she didn't dare turn, didn't dare look at him. Matthieu was behind her and even through the distance between them she felt it. The shock, the grief, the anger, the pain… She soaked it up like a sponge, consuming it and letting that too wash over her.

An electronic sound of a picture being taken followed only moments behind the blinding flash and Maria flinched at both. Her eyes took a second to adjust, even though she had turned her face in the direction of the photographer only feet away.

Within seconds, several flashes stuttered into the room and Matthieu had stalked past her to thrust the man up against a white wall, their dark-suited figures stark in contrast. Angry incomprehensible words echoed within the empty gallery, security guards rushing in to drag the men apart.

Matthieu pulled away from the guard, speaking so quickly, Maria could barely translate. Not that she needed to. His tone was indication enough. From behind him, the photographer was pointing and yelling at her husband and, without sparing the man another glace, Matthieu turned on his heel and stalked from the room.

With his departure, the chain holding her still lifted and she practically ran after Matthieu, chasing the sounds of his fast footsteps as he left the exhibition. She passed Margery, barely registering the woman's distress, leaving her behind, and followed as Matthieu left the building through a discreet doorway and made his way out into the gardens of the museum, her heels plunging into the thick grass making her steps harder, as if even the ground were trying to hold her back from reaching him in that moment.

In very little time they reached a small helicopter and while the pilot frantically readied the aircraft, Matthieu held the door back to her with barely leashed emotion that had gripped his entire body in such a way that she dared not speak.

She climbed into the helicopter, quickly assuring herself that it was safe to fly at this stage of her pregnancy, and slid over to the far side to make room for Matthieu. But instead of joining her, he closed the door and slipped into the seat next to the now ready pilot.

Maria could have moved back into the middle but she didn't. Instead, she stayed in the far corner, clinging to the edge of the seat as the helicopter jerked up from the ground before sweeping up into the night sky.

Everything around her was dark, the mood, the light, the landscape beneath her. Shadows and little dots of lights punctured the thick, midnight blanket that had enveloped her, but did nothing to soothe the guilt that wracked her from head to toe. That the photographer had caught Matthieu at such a vulnerable moment, such an exposed, raw, heartbreaking moment... It had been the first time she had seen even a glimpse of the extent of her husband's pain.

Maria hadn't known her mother. She had died bringing her into this world, and Maria had inherited only memories from her brother and father to guide her in shaping an impression of the woman who had given birth to her. Maria's pain was more like that of a phantom limb, itching and aching in a way that was absent, rather than real. Yes, she had felt loss and anger and frustration, but in a slightly removed way, as if never really quite sure what she was missing.

But for Matthieu it was different. So very different.

It felt as if they had been flying for both an age and no time at all. Maria was pulled from her thoughts as the helicopter dropped gently on the helipad at the back of the estate in Lucerne she vaguely remembered seeing from one of her walks.

Although everything in her wanted to fling back the door and flee into the night, she wasn't sure of the safety protocol and only then did she realise she'd had her first flight in a helicopter, so lost had she been in her thoughts. Thoughts of him, thoughts of her.

The door slid back and Matthieu's shadowed, brooding form beckoned her forth. She picked up her skirts and hunched within the low interior, stepped out and followed his retreating form. As she followed him through the darkness, with the sounds of the helicopter's engine receding behind her, she heard the ping of Matthieu's phone. Once, twice. A brief pause between a third and fourth. But he ignored it in the same way that he was ignoring her.

And suddenly she was angry. Angry that he could not even bring himself to look at her, let alone speak to her. The closer and closer they got to the estate, the more furious she became, feeling a little as if she was being brought back to a prison.

A prison where her husband barely tolerated her presence. There were times in her childhood when she'd

felt extreme loneliness—while her father, stepmother
and brother argued about money behind closed doors,
'adult' business that didn't involve her. Decisions being
made about their future, her future, ones she had no
say in. She had once promised herself not to ever be in
that position again. And the one time she had chosen
something for herself, the one time she had followed
her instincts, the consequences had seen her right back
behind another set of closed doors, under the control
of her husband.

He led them back into the house through the door
from the garden and stalked into the open-plan kitchen
and living room, but this time when Matthieu turned
towards his office, the doorway she never breached, she
couldn't take it any more. She knew he was angry, furious even, but she would not live in silence, she would
not allow herself to avoid this any longer.

'Ask me why I went to the gala tonight,' she called
out to him.

He halted, his hand outstretched towards the door
handle. She could tell he was warring within himself,
to push on forwards into the room he would close himself off in, or to turn and give into her demand. She
only exhaled as she saw the tense outline of his shoulders turn and she finally locked eyes with her husband.

'Why did you go to the gala tonight, Maria?' His
tone was droll and mechanical. Purposely so and it
made her mad. Seething frustration and anger that she
just couldn't get through to him. Couldn't get past the
barriers he had built between them.

'I went because Mrs Montcour had been invited to a gala and I wanted to see her.'

He frowned. 'You're not making sense.'

She practically growled out loud, only just managing to resist the urge to stamp her foot. 'I went because I didn't know who I was as your wife. Maria Rohan de Luen? Yes, I was actually just getting to know her before this. She was just beginning to find her freedom. Just beginning to make her own decisions and choices,' she said, desperate to explain, to reach him, to make a connection. 'But Maria Montcour? She's new to me. I went to the gala because I wanted to see who she was, to see if she was different perhaps, more confident… more powerful even? And maybe, *just maybe*, going to a gala organised by a charity founded by my husband, whether he was present or not, would help me see a little more about who he is, what makes him tick, other than that he has a penchant for concrete!' She hadn't meant to shout, but that was where her little speech had ended. Her shouting at him. She didn't think she'd ever shouted at anyone before in her life.

For a moment, she thought that her words had no effect. None at all. He might as well have been made of the concrete he'd made his house from. His phone pinged another few times, cutting through the silence between them.

'Well, you certainly got to see that. And so did the press,' he growled. 'Did you not think?' he demanded, spinning around to turn on her. 'About how tonight was everything I had wanted to avoid for nearly *ten*

years? I tried to warn you about the press, about what
vultures they are and how they would do anything to
get even just a glimpse of the *beast* and the innocent
now tied to him.'

Maria's heart broke just a little at his words. Was
that truly how he saw them?

'The moment you stepped out on the red carpet the
entire world knew that you were married to me and
pregnant with my child.'

'I'll concede that perhaps I hadn't quite thought it
through.'

'We don't have the luxury of not thinking it through.
Not now.'

'Matthieu, the press were always going to find out,'
she said gently but persistently.

'At a time of our choosing. Not one that would impact upon the charity!'

'Matthieu—' Yet another ping emitted from his
phone, cutting through her words. 'Oh, for God's sake,
what is wrong with your phone?' she demanded.

'Do you really have no idea?' he returned, seemingly incredulous. 'Here,' he said, sweeping a thumb
across his phone before passing it to her. 'Take a look.'

As she held the phone in her hand, scrolling down
through page after page of social media headlines about
the beast showing his colours, the beast wedding an
innocent, the beast's secret violence, some questioning if Maria was safe, the more ridiculous pondering
whether she had been kidnapped, her fingers began
to shake. Yes, there were a few positive ones, about

how Matthieu Montcour had found his happy-ever-after, about the resounding success of the charity gala's event, the joy at the future heir to the Montcour dynasty, but her thumb stalled over the last image captured on his phone. The image of Matthieu standing behind Maria, her hand over her mouth in shock, the glistening of tears in her eyes as they both took in the painting of Matthieu and his parents. And the violation of that moment devastated her because in all her attempts of finding herself, she had brought the wolf directly to Matthieu's door.

CHAPTER SEVEN

MATTHIEU WAS FURIOUS. With the press, with Maria, with himself. For the first time in his life he couldn't blame someone else. He was the one who had truly lived up to his reputation as a beast the moment he had pushed the photographer up against the wall. It was his actions, his loss of control that had furthered the obscene attention-grabbing headlines.

Before the gala he had set his phone to notify him of any social media posts relating to him or Maria. And the phone gripped tight in Maria's slightly shaking hands was still pinging away.

Because he had lost control. Because that damn photographer had caught them, caught *him*, with his defences down and it had allowed all the anger and the violence out.

He closed his eyes, but the family portrait his father had commissioned months before the night of the fire was imprinted on his mind. He conceded that the artistry was perfect. Because the hours that must have gone into creating such a masterpiece had truly caught the truth of his family. The joy and love shining from their eyes, made so much more invaluable by the events that followed, had been too much. Too much and not enough. He'd barely remembered it being done because he rarely allowed memories of before to pass beyond the steel door he'd shut upon them once he'd left hospital. Because if he hadn't, he truly wasn't sure he'd have survived.

And now that he had seen it, now that memories were beginning to seep through the small gap that had been opened just a few hours ago, Matthieu slammed the vault door shut, hoping that it would be enough, hoping that he'd done so in time.

'Matthieu—'

'I warned you. I warned you what would happen but you went anyway!' He hated that he was shouting. Hated that he was still trying to wrestle his control back into place.

'I didn't... I'm sorry.'

'Your apology means nothing,' he bit out cruelly. 'I need you to understand. Understand that this is what it is like for me. Understand that this is what it is like to be married to me and what it is and will be like for you and for our child. That always the paparazzi will be stalking us, following our every move. Our every moment. They always have, ever since...'

He flinched the moment she laid a hand on his arm, trying to turn him to face her, and it took everything in him not to shake it off. Because she did need to understand. He needed to make her. That the world would never tire of the tragedy that was his past, never tire of the beast that was his present.

'After the funerals, I missed most of the press furore. Malcolm and the hospital managed to keep it away from me then. So I wasn't prepared for what happened. But I need you to be.'

'What happened, Matthieu?'

Matthieu blew out a breath. Resenting that he was about to open this wound for her, but knowing that it was better than the deeper hurt. Better than the hurt that he'd just locked behind the steel trap in his mind. 'Do you know how I first earned my reputation as a beast? The scars were one thing, but I was seventeen the first time they coined that phrase.' He turned then, because he needed her to see.

She was staring up at him, so small, so perfect, so fragile.

'Malcolm had wanted me to have something of a normal life,' he explained. A cynical huff of laughter escaped his lungs and bled hurt into the air between them. 'By seventeen I was finally well enough to attend school, but it was difficult. I'd been amongst adults, nurses, doctors, and private teachers for six years by that point. I had very little experience of being around people my age. Teenagers who had already formed friend groups and cliques. So I kept to myself. Head down, studied. Because of my private education I was put ahead a year and was already an oddity, and the scars? They proved more of a curiosity amongst the students than I had ever imagined. When one of the prettiest girls in the school asked me to help her with her studies, I…' He spared barely a sigh for the naïve young boy he'd been then. 'I had thought she might be different. When I realised that she was flirting with me, I was astounded, eager…desperate even.' He closed his eyes against the memories of those naïve fumblings, the sting of anger towards Clara never having gone away. Instead, turning into a lesson he revisited whenever he felt weak.

The self-recrimination, the *humiliation* of how innocent he had been was like a knife twisting in his gut. But he had to continue. Maria had to understand. 'In such a short time, she'd orchestrated my feelings like a maestro. I thought myself half in love and would have given her anything. She was very clear on what she wanted from me, and I knew no better. Until that point, no one had seen my scars. I had never done any sports, worn my school jumper even in the heights of summer. I should have known,' he said more to himself than to Maria. He turned away, casting his gaze into the night, but couldn't avoid the reflection of her face in the glass window. He could tell that she had a sense of what he was about to say. Could see, feel even, the sympathy, the concern, passing from herself to him. He shook it off and pressed on.

'She had a camera. I didn't know. She and her friends had been approached by an unscrupulous journalist who had offered them an obscene amount of money for a picture of me. But that wasn't enough for Clara. She arranged a greater pay-out for an accompanying article about how I had seduced her and tried to take advantage of her. About how I had grown angry when she wouldn't do what I wanted. A harsh irony because I had been the one to refuse to sleep with her, wanting to take things slowly. As if being rejected by a beast like me had burned her ego. Malcolm had an injunction taken out, the article didn't make publication, but it was too late. Rumours filled the school, reaching the parents, reaching the press…the damage had been done.'

Maria was shaking. With fury, with injustice… For the first time *she* felt like the beast, wanting to lash out and destroy. That such a thing had been done to him. That he had been so badly misused and betrayed, on top of the devastation that he had already experienced. Suddenly memories of their first night together crashed down upon her. It must have taken so much for him to give into her request It must have taken trust. A trust that she hadn't earned then, but wanted to now. She wanted him to see what she saw.

'I am truly sorry that happened to you.'

He shrugged his shoulder, as if dismissing her and the compassion she offered. But she wouldn't be dismissed. Not this time. She turned him around to face her and waited until he met her eyes.

'But you need to know that I did not and *do* not see you as a beast. And…' She paused, hoping that Matthieu would understand, would believe her next words. 'And I think you should also know that not all the posts on your phone, not all the press reports, do either.'

He scoffed and turned back away from her. She didn't need his phone to remember the other headlines.

Montcour Finds Happiness.

Montcour's Charity a Resounding Success.

Millions Raised by Montcour.

'Matthieu—did you ever think that the reason the press are so interested in you is not because of the scars, or your reputation, or the loss of your family, but because you survived? Because you turned something truly terrible into something amazing? A charity that gives back to those that need it?'

Disbelief and something painfully like hope shone in his eyes. It gave her the strength to carry on.

'That they aren't horrified, but amazed by how well you've done for yourself?'

He frowned and in that moment she wondered whether he had even seen those particular headlines amongst the dross that had spewed onto social media.

She could see him trying to assimilate what she had said into how he had spent years of his life viewing the negative headlines about him and what he'd achieved. She could almost feel the war within him as he tried to reframe the image of himself, not through the bitter lens of the desperate press, but as how she saw him, as how others might. But before she could tell what conclusion he had come to, he shut down. She could almost hear the door closing on his thoughts.

'I am going to bed.'

And he left her standing alone in the middle of the large open space, concrete and soft white leather, so stark in comparison to the way his entire being had become her sole focus, the large, heated breath of his body… She couldn't leave it like that. Couldn't just let him walk away. He was in pain, that she could see clearly. For a while she simply stood there, wanting to go to him, not sure if she had that right. But if she didn't, she saw how their future would be—two isolated and lonely people sharing the same space, the same love for a child, but not together. If she let him go this night, she suddenly felt that she would lose Matthieu for ever.

She followed the path he had taken up the stairs to the bedrooms, the one she had been allocated all the way at the other end of the house—as if as far away from him as possible. But she would not retreat, would not hide, would not abandon him tonight.

She pushed open the door to his room, the one she had never been in or seen. For a moment she was plunged back to the night they had spent in Iondorra. His room was just as large, almost big enough to contain the entire flat she had shared with Evin and Anita in Camberwell.

It was beautiful. The bed jutted out, as if floating inches above the floor, the frame and headboard made from reclaimed oak, warming the incredible breadth of the side wall that met floor-to-ceiling windows framed in black, making the most of the stunning view of Lake Lucerne, even in the night time. It must be incredible in the morning, Maria thought. Either side of the inconceivably large bed hung a series of metal tubes, like huge wind-chimes, glowing gently with discreet

lighting. Behind her the entire wall was encased in an-
tique mirror, flooding her mind with shockingly sensual thoughts as to what might be seen from the bed,
bringing an almost painful blush to her cheeks.

From the corner of the room was a corridor that
must have led immediately into the bathroom, because
she could hear the sounds of water streaming from a
shower, traces of steam tinged with the scent of lemon
grass reached where she stood.

She slipped off her shoes and made her way towards
the shower, swirls and twists in the steam beckoning
her forth. The long swathes of heavy silky material
sweeping behind her bare feet made a gentle brushing
sound that barely reached her ears.

As she rounded the corner, the sight took her breath
away. Hidden lighting illuminated the space in long
strips, copper taps and accents warmed the grey tones
of the concrete, and the glass-fronted shower unit, large
enough for more people than Maria dared to imagine in
a shower, was only partially misted. Behind the glass
she could see Matthieu, his head bent under the powerful jets of water, his arms outstretched against the
wall as if he was bracing himself against the emotions
of that night. For just a moment she allowed herself to
watch as the water cascaded over the stunning breadth
of his shoulders, the way it twisted over his muscles,
as if it clung to his skin until it had traversed as much
of the length of him as possible. Her fingers itched to
follow its path across his skin, back and down to his
legs and calves. She had never been so enthralled by

a man—not even her naïve crush on Theo had been this devastating.

She fumbled with the fastening at the back of her dress but her fingers caught against the clasp and the urgency to go to him increased with each heartbeat to the point where she couldn't care less about the dress. Refusing to waste any time, she reached for the handle and swept aside the glass, catching his image in the reflection and noting that Matthieu's only reaction was a raised eyebrow, nothing else. Not even a turn of his head, not even the stiffening of his shoulders. Just a simple wry questioning gesture that barely acknowledged her presence.

But she would not be ignored. Not in this. Not now and not ever again.

She picked up her skirts, stepped over the threshold of the shower fully clothed, and ducked beneath one powerful arm, to bring herself in between them, facing him. He yanked his head back, finally unable to escape or deny her.

'What are you doing?' he demanded, but left his arms where they were, still braced against the wall, encasing her, as if perhaps teasing or testing himself, she couldn't tell.

The water soaked into the dress, making it impossibly heavy, but she didn't care. It turned her hair into thick ropes that broke free from the pins that had held them in place and fell around her shoulders and down her back. But all she wanted, all she could think of was his hands on her skin, the feel of him beneath her tongue, and touch. She reached up and cupped his jaw, running her thumb over the rich dark beard that was surprising in its softness. She gazed up at him as rivers of water poured over them both, each now breathing as hard as if they'd run a marathon.

'You need this. *I* need this,' she said before sweeping her hand around his neck and pulling him down to meet her lips, just as she said, '*We* need this.'

The moment his lips pressed against hers, Matthieu's mind and heart were consumed with need. She might have offered an alternative vision of how the press viewed him, but how he had viewed *her* had not once changed. She was irresistible. Her soft, wet slicked skin, the plumpness of her lips, he wanted it all. He braced himself against the cool concrete of the shower enclosure and devoured her, his tongue plunging deep, teeth gently scraping against the softness of her. Her hands were wrapped around his neck, clinging to him as much as he wanted to cling to her, her breasts moulded against his chest, bump against abdomen. He held himself back, bridged against the wall, yet consumed everything she could offer him with her mouth, her touch. He could have sworn he was shaking with the effort of fighting the need for restraint and the desire for more.

For an entire month he had avoided this, avoided her. Not because he hadn't wanted her. But because he had. Because he'd wanted her with such a raw need that it had threatened to undo him. But after tonight, after all the emotions dredged up from where he had kept them locked and hidden away, by both the press and the painting, he wasn't strong enough to deny him, *them*, this. And damn him, but he was going to take everything she had to give.

'The baby?' he said, the last barrier to lifting the leash on his desires completely.

'Will be absolutely fine,' she assured him, pressing another kiss to his lips. And it was the sweetest thing he thought he'd ever heard.

Leaning back and pulling one hand from the wall, he wrapped it around her back, bringing her closer to him, pressing her against the length of him, bringing a half laugh from deep within his chest. 'You're still wearing your dress.'

'What are you going to do about it?' she demanded, not full of coquettish intonation. More of a challenge— a challenge and a silent demand.

He wanted to growl and beat his chest, not like the beast she denied that he was, but the animal she was turning him into being. He wanted to tear it from her body. As the water cascaded down from above, he loosened his hold on the wall and reached down to fist the layers of material by her thigh. The soaking wet bundle leached more water, pooling over his hand and down his arm. He released his hold on the material and reached for what he really wanted. Her.

'Turn around,' he commanded and, casting him a look of sheer unwarranted trust, she did, turning her head to the side and exposing the long thin column of her neck to the hot sprays, causing her hair to dip and fall over one shoulder. Between her shoulder blades where each side of the dress gathered was the top of the zip. His fingers went to it and slowly, oh, so slowly, drew the tab down from the top, the weight of the waterlogged silks pulling the dress apart, exposing the length of her spine, the curve just beneath his fingertips so that he was unable to stop himself from tracing the progress with his thumb. She shivered beneath his touch and he wanted more. So he pressed openmouthed kisses across the skin of her back, delighting and devouring in each inch that was revealed to him.

With one arm wrapped around her, covering her breasts, and the other drawing the zip down to the base of her spine, he felt as if he held the most precious thing in the world in his arms and that he was not, and never could be, worthy of such a thing.

She arched into his touch, as if desperate to feel more, and he could not deny her any longer. Slowly, he turned her in his arms, gazing into the dark brown orbs that studied him with an intensity he felt deep within him. He watched as she lifted a hand and brushed the material of the dress off her shoulders, fascinated as it poured from her skin, and she was left standing before him in nothing more than her panties, rivulets of water glistening trails of silver across creamy skin that he wanted to trace with his tongue.

She reached for his hands and pulled them gently around her belly and his thoughts splintered between the firmness of the slightly strange shapes beneath his

palms and the fact that their child was within her, protected by her, loved by them both. He worried about his
hands, so large, and Maria and their child so small. And
she smiled up at him as if sharing the same thought.

'Surrounded by us both,' she whispered to him
above the pounding of the water around them. Was it
wrong to want such carnal things from his wife when
she was pregnant with his child? he wondered. Ever
since Clara, he'd always believed that intimacy needed
to be emotionless, no expectation of hope or betrayal,
desires simply and easily requested or refused—no
judgement or pressure. But this? This sense of attach-
ment to his wife was threatening to cut him off at the
knees.

Because suddenly his needs and wants didn't matter—all that mattered was Maria and what she wanted
and desired and how he could give them to her. When
she had come into his shower, all he had wanted was
to erase the night, to delve into sensual satisfaction that
would rob him of thought and want, but now? Now he
didn't care if he lived on a rack of his emotions for the
next twenty years of his life. All he wanted was her to
have every indulgence, every desire, want and need
met and exceeded.

He hooked a thumb into the side of her panties,
slowly drawing the material down over her hips and
thighs, and pushing them to the floor. With one hand,
he reached for her neck, pulling her into a kiss as he
delved between her legs with the other, drawing a gasp
from her lips, one that he immediately consumed, pull-

ing her breath deep within him, wanting everything, her moans, her cries of pleasure. Almost instantly she bucked against his hand, quivering with unchecked arousal that matched his own. He felt the tremor run across her skin beneath the layer of slick water that poured down from above them. He cursed, so close she was to orgasm that he feared it would call forth his own. His hard erection jutted against the smooth firm curve of her abdomen, again and again as her moans grew sensually urgent and full with need.

Words, begging and pleading, fell from her lips and he wanted to give her everything. He dropped to his knees, supporting her with his hands around her backside, the glorious feel of it filling the palms of his hands, more exquisite than he could have imagined.

He followed the path of his thumb across her clitoris with his tongue and he preened beneath the stifled moan of pleasure that her hand blocked from leaving her mouth. Ruthlessly he drove her to the edge and back, over and over again, because he wanted, needed, her as lost in her passion as he was.

As her cries mounted, so did his need, but he held himself firmly in check, because it was no longer about him and his wants, but her. She came apart in his hands and mouth and he had never experienced anything more magnificent or beautiful in his life.

Maria was shaking and she didn't care, clinging to Matthieu's shoulders as if it were the only way she could remain standing. *Standing.* She had come to him for his needs and he had seen only to her own, but couldn't find it within herself to feel regret and instead focused on the soaring pleasure shimmering through her body.

She had thought that she'd imagined it, misremembered the dizzying heights Matthieu had taken her to that night almost five months ago now. But she hadn't. Instead, she wondered whether time had in fact dulled her memory because every touch, kiss, caress rang through her body like a song—the melody both familiar and yet strangely new and wonderful.

She let her head fall back as warm water cascaded over her. Matthieu rose and took her in his arms in a way she'd only dreamed of.

'You look like a mermaid,' he said, the honey-coloured glint in his eye highlighted by the surrounding emerald green.

'A large, round, pregnant mermaid?'

'You look incredible.'

'Smooth talker,' she said, gently slapping him on the shoulder, the wet of their skin making the sound louder than she'd expected.

'Hardly,' he admitted, his voice gravelly. He reached out a finger to loop beneath the silver necklace that hung between her bare breasts. 'You are always wearing this.'

'It is the only thing I have left of my mother,' she replied. 'She died bringing me into this world.'

Matthieu's breath left his chest on a *whoosh*, and he closed his eyes against her words. 'Maria... I am so sorry.'

And she gently smiled as if trying to ease his sympathetic ache. 'Had it not been for me, she would have lived. Sebastian would have had a mother and my father wouldn't have hidden his grief in apathy, a second wife who would rather spend money than love us, and risky business deals that almost destroyed us.' She placed a hand on his arm. 'I don't blame myself. I can't. I know that it's not my fault, that there was nothing I could have done, that I was a baby. She had a medical complication. But I do know something of loss, Matthieu.'

The words came unbidden to his lips.

'I am glad you have this. That you are able to have it with you. The only thing I have left...' He paused, the stab of pain stark and foreign yet somehow strangely familiar. 'The only thing I have that belonged to my parents is the present my mother gave to my father the night they died. It was their twelfth wedding anniversary, and she had given him the gift just before my bedtime.' His breathing became hard, as he remembered what had happened later, but forced himself back to the present. 'It's burned, mostly melted and deeply damaged by the fire.'

Maria frowned. 'Where is it?'

He shrugged his shoulder as if it were nothing, when it was everything. 'In my bedside cabinet.'

Matthieu looked at her then and saw what he had feared since the first moment he'd caught sight of her. Somehow he'd known, even then, that she would unearth his grief, his pain...understand it even. That she would be the one to break down the walls around his heart. Walls that he had relied on for the last twenty years. Walls that he didn't know how to live without. Because that would mean opening himself up…leaving himself vulnerable to the same kind of loss that nearly destroyed him once before.

She kissed him then, one of compassion, one of sympathy and understanding that he feared she might not want to have given when she discovered the truth about the present and what it had cost his entire family. Coward that he was, he lost himself in that kiss, deliberately stoking its fire, rousing the passion between them.

'Matthieu—' Her words cut off in a squeal as he picked her up entirely and took them both from the shower. Her cries turned into giggles as he set her on her feet and dried her in the most gloriously fluffy towel she'd ever touched.

'Maria Montcour, this is absolutely no laughing matter. I take my duties very seriously.'

At his half jokingly stern words, the laughter dimmed in her mind. 'I know,' she said, and couldn't help the vein of sadness running through her words. She knew he did and would. Because of who he was, because of what had happened to him, because that was the man he had become. But perhaps…not because of her.

She pushed aside the thought and reached to caress his jaw. This man who had offered her compassion and understanding for her own loss, when he seemed to hide from his own. She loved the feel of the firm proud line of it, covered by the soft swirls of the short beard he kept. Her heart leapt as he leant into her touch and placed a kiss on the palm of her hand. Then her wrist, and then down the inside of her forearm.

Surely it was wrong to want someone so much so soon after—

Her brain almost short-circuited as his thumb outlined the curve of her breast—her body so extremely sensitive and responsive since the pregnancy.

As he ran the pad of his thumb over her already taut nipple she fought the moan of pleasure that started deep within her. 'Bed. Now,' she commanded, wondering when she had become so empowered.

'As you wish,' he replied, sweeping her up off her feet and walking them to the bed where he gently laid her down and got in beside her.

Maria would remember that night for the rest of her life. Their lovemaking became just that. Loving, giving and receiving, pleasure almost indescribable as they each reached the heights of an impossible rapture. Neither were held back by doubts, or haunted by what was to come, both instead lost in pure unadulterated, endless unchecked bliss.

CHAPTER EIGHT

MARIA DIDN'T KNOW what she had expected following the night of the gala. Perhaps for her new life to go back to the strange untouched isolation that she had experienced after the wedding…but she couldn't have been more wrong.

On the first night she'd gone to her room only for Matthieu to stalk in, pick her up off the bed, carry her to his, gently lay her down on the bed and get in beside her. All without saying a word. It happened again on the second night and Maria was too confused to want to break the strange spell that had descended on them with questions or words.

On the third night, when the baby had been un-settled and sleep elusive, he had turned on the dim lighting, lain on his side facing her and asked her how she'd made her first piece of jewellery. He'd peppered her with questions about each and every step until she had fallen asleep in the middle of an explanation about the small forge that she had used in the studio in Camberwell.

Matthieu did it again on the fourth and fifth night until Maria was half convinced that he'd be able to make the perfect bracelet without ever once having touched the tools and materials he'd need.

He hadn't touched her, though. Hadn't recreated the intimacies of the night of the gala and that was becoming pure torture for her. Days spent wondering, questioning, doubting… Had she imagined the connection she had felt forged the night of the gala? Had it just been what they'd needed in that moment? But if that was the case, then why would he bring her to his room each and every night…?

Each day, while he retreated to his office in Zürich, Maria walked the forests around the lake, losing herself in the beauty of the surrounding areas, the crunch of leaves beneath her feet, and the soft gentle heat of the departing summer. And each day she marvelled at the changes to her body and the child she carried. Her hands smoothed down the rounded shape hanging low within her, the weight and stretch catching her both by surprise and with something like awe. For the first time in her life, Maria had begun to wonder about her mother—as if her own pregnancy had soothed aside the hurt, and replaced it with a curious yearning ache for something she could never have, and never know.

But the tightening of clothes that had only been purchased a month before made Maria realise that she would need to return to the shops once more, her mind calculating what resources she had in her savings and hating the fact that she would either have to turn to her husband or brother for more money. Neither of which was a particularly pleasant option. For so long she had tried so hard to find her own independence, and now? She felt utterly trapped by a man who was so complicated, so tormented by his own past, yet also by a man she was beginning to see as something more than just the autocratic, albeit devastatingly attractive, isolated man she had married.

Though trapped was too simple a word to describe what her life had become. Because she did have her freedoms and, more, his focus. At night, they had begun to talk less of jewellery and more of hopes and dreams…names for the baby, plans for its future. All of which painted a picture that Maria feared was more spellbound than real, as if one wrong turn and it could vanish in the air like a wisp of autumnal mist.

She reached a part of the woodland that broke over the stunning view of Lake Lucerne towards the edge of Matthieu's property and let out a weighted sigh, lost in the way the horizon met the mirror-smooth lake, the parallel beauty of two shades of blue so close they seemed two halves of the same whole. Something would break the harmony she'd discovered in the last week, whether it was her, Matthieu or someone else, she was sure of it. The fragile détente they had found between them…it just couldn't last.

She returned from her walk, her muscles pleasantly aching, the pressure from the too-small waistband not so much. She reached for her phone, determined to find some better-fitting clothes online, when she saw the screen display fifteen missed calls from her brother. Fear spiked through her mind, which panicked while she hit the call button and waited to be connected to Sebastian.

Come on, come on, pick up.

When she heard his gruff voice answer she barrelled questions at him in rapid fire.

'What's wrong? Has something happened? Are you okay?'

'I don't know, sis. You tell me.'

'What?' Maria asked, dropping into the chair by the table, relieved at least that he sounded okay.

'Well, I don't hear from you for a couple of months—perhaps not so unusual given your tendency to get lost in some project or other—'

Maria couldn't help but flinch at the way Seb dismissed her work.

'And then… Bam. There you are, front cover of over fifteen different magazines in several different languages, looking *decidedly* pregnant and apparently very much married? So you tell me if something "is wrong", if something "has happened", and by God, Maria, if you are okay!'

Maria knew on some level she had been blocking thoughts of Seb from her mind. Unable to find the words to explain. And she suddenly realised that she'd plunged her head in the sand and tried to ignore the reality of it all. Was this what was going to break the spell between her and Matthieu? Harsh reality?

'Seb, I—'

Her brother's exhale was harsh and loud in her ear. 'You said you were in Switzerland visiting "a friend",' he accused. 'Please, Maria, just tell me you're okay.'

'I am,' she assured him. 'Truly, I am.'

Over the next half an hour she lied to her brother— something she'd never done before—weaving a veil of fiction so thin over the way she had met and married Matthieu she could almost see the truth through it. But no matter what she said, it wasn't enough. Sebastian wanted to see her, to meet Matthieu, and Maria wasn't able to refuse the invitation, which was more of an ultimatum, to attend a dinner at his estate just outside Siena in a couple of days' time. And suddenly thoughts and fears cascaded through her mind on an endless loop.

By the time Matthieu pulled into the sweeping drive of his estate, he wasn't sure whether he wanted to swing the car round and drive away, or throw the car into park and rush towards the wife he couldn't quite figure out.

Ever since the night of the gala, he'd been unable— no, unwilling—to sleep in a bed without his wife. And he couldn't explain it. It had just felt...wrong. The moment he'd taken her to his bed, he'd felt something shift within him, something that soothed the raging beast in a way he'd never experienced. It wasn't her touch, her cries of pleasure. Unsettlingly it had nothing to do with the incredible heights of passion they'd shared. No, worse—it seemed that it was her mere presence that calmed him in a way nothing before ever had. Each night, when she couldn't sleep, he'd asked her questions…just to hear the sound of her voice. He'd lie awake at night, just watching the rise and fall of her chest, and their child that was to be. Because the night of the gala, the way she had brushed past the dark headlines and focused on the good ones, she had shown him something that he'd never seen before. *Survivor.* The word still rang round his head, making him wonder if that was how their child might see him, making him *want* it.

He stalked down the hallway, frowning as he heard Maria's steps taking her, what sounded like, back and forth. Matthieu was well versed in the patterns of pacing and was already frowning as he rounded the corner to find Maria turning on her heel, and twisting her hands round each other.

'What's wrong?'

She looked up, startled and almost guilty, then turned back to her pacing.

'Maria?'

She shrugged a shoulder, aiming for nonchalant, he presumed, and failing miserably. 'Oh, you know.'

'No… I don't, which is why I asked.'

She batted a hand in his direction without stopping her passage back and forth in the living area. If she didn't stop she was going to make him— Fear, sudden and crashing, carved a jagged wound in his heart. 'The baby—?'

'Oh, God, no. Fine, the baby is fine,' she said, stopping the movement of her feet and looking half appalled that he might have thought such a thing, before resuming her pacing.

His heart juddered and he took a few deep breaths to try and pull back the raging speed it had leapt to.

'It's just that…my brother… We have to go to Italy, and I'm not sure I'm ready for that. I don't even have the right clothes and—'

He couldn't help let out a laugh, now that he knew there was nothing wrong with their child, as he struggled to understand the chain of her thoughts.

'What do clothes have to do with Italy and your brother?'

'He knows, Matthieu. He saw a photo of us at the gala. A very pregnant, married "us".'

'You didn't tell him?'

'I…'

Matthieu felt his frown return. It wasn't as if they'd actually talked that much about her family. He knew she had a brother, that her father had remarried after the loss of his first wife in childbirth with Maria. Had he just assumed that she had told them? Perhaps he had assumed a little too much where his wife was concerned.

'What did he say?'

'He wants us to visit him in Siena. He wants…to meet you.'

Matthieu managed to resist the urge to laugh this time. Clearly this meant a lot to Maria. He'd never seen her like this before—all this buzzing energy and indecision. Casting his mind back, he was pretty sure that she'd been less panicked when telling him that she was pregnant.

'Then we'll go,' he said simply. And for the first time she stopped pacing.

'Really?'

'Yes, Maria. He's your family, it's important.' Good God, did she think he was a monster that would refuse to visit her brother? But rather than seem relieved, she turned a lighter shade of pale and Matthieu sensed that there was definitely something more going on.

'But I have nothing to wear,' she cried.

His eyebrows shot up—he was sure he could feel them disappearing into his hairline. When had Maria ever cared about clothing?

'Maria—'

'And shoes! My shoes don't even fit right now, because I'm just getting…fat. Everywhere. In places that aren't around my child. And don't,' she said, spinning back to him and pointing a stabbing finger in his direction, 'don't for one minute dare to even *think* that this is *hormones*,' she hissed.

'I didn't—'

'Because, yes, there are hormones, lots of them!' She was most definitely shouting now, and in that moment Matthieu was regretting the smooth planes of concrete he had loved so much and was yearning for soft furnishings to take the edge off the anger vibrating around the room. 'So many. Making me want to eat ice cream. All. The. Time. Surely that's what morning sickness is there for? To balance the scales. Why couldn't I just have morning sickness?'

'You want—'

'Of course I don't want to be sick, don't be ridiculous.'

Matthieu couldn't tell whether he wanted to laugh or cry, and sensed more than anything that Maria was also torn between the two. But he was now convinced that although there might be something to the hormones, it wasn't everything and if he didn't do something this conversation would end very badly indeed.

He stalked over to the freezer and hunted in the bottom drawer to find what he was looking for. He seized it with one hand and riffled in the cutlery drawer for a spoon. Returning to the small island that he strategically placed between him and his rather adorably flustered, but most definitely volatile wife, he took off the lid of the ice-cream pot.

'What are you doing?' she asked.

'Eating.' He plunged the spoon into the depths of the carton and retrieved a sizable amount and consumed the entire mouthful.

'Now? You're eating now? When I've just—'

'From now on,' he said, around a mouthful of the cold sweet dessert and swallowing, whilst digging around for another spoonful, 'I eat what you eat.' He stared at her with determination and watched her expressive features as they shifted focus from whatever crazy chain of thought she'd been on, to watching him eat spoonful after spoonful of ice cream. Only, he realised too late, he was about to get brain freeze. No matter. He'd eat the whole damn tub if it would make her feel better right now.

He waited until he was sure that he had her full attention. 'So we're going to Italy?'

'Sebastian has invited us for dinner at his in two days' time.'

'Okay, I'll clear my schedule. You're okay to fly?'

'Yes?'

'We'll take the jet,' he said, and although another mouthful of ice cream was the last thing he ever wanted to see again in his life, he pushed another spoonful in his mouth. He'd been deadly serious about his declaration.

'You...you don't mind?' she asked tentatively and Matthieu hated the thought that she was afraid to ask. Not just in this, but afraid to ask something that was so clearly important to her.

'Not at all. Not if you don't mind telling me what's really going on here,' he said as his stomach began to freeze from the inside out from all the ice cream. He nearly laughed as he watched her eyes lock onto the spoon he was about to put into his mouth. 'Would you like some?'

She clenched her jaw and seemingly tried to hold herself back, until he finally watched her give in. Her shoulders dropped and she closed the distance to the island counter.

'Yes.'

'Yes you mind? Yes you want some?'

'Yes to both?' she asked, not quite meeting his gaze.

* * *

Maria sighed. From the moment Matthieu had returned home, her mouth had run away with her and her mind was hurling everything and anything into her thoughts to prevent her from facing the one thing she didn't want to face, but in reality probably really needed to.

'When did you get so wise?' she asked Matthieu.

'Probably around the time my wife said, *"You need this. I need this. We need this."*'

In an instant she was plunged back into the sensations he had wrought to her body that night. The need, the passion…

'Mind out of the gutter, wife.'

'My hormones have a lot to answer for.'

'And I promise, when we've had this discussion, your hormones can feast on my body until they're sated,' he growled, the dark promise in his eyes almost too much to bear.

'Really?' she said uncertainly. 'Because you haven't…we haven't…since that night.'

He sighed and she felt the gentle puff of air against her skin, sweet with the taste of ice cream.

He placed the spoon down on the counter and she reached for it, even though her stomach had finally revolted and given up any desire for food—or at least *that* kind of feasting.

He ran his hands through his hair and finally leaned on one elbow, resting his chin in his palm and looking at her as if he'd given up some kind of internal fight. 'Honestly, I wasn't sure that was something you wanted. I didn't want you to feel that because of that night, I automatically assumed that…'

'My husband could demand his nightly conjugal rights?' she finished with a small sad smile. When had things got so complicated that they couldn't simply act on their desires, or feelings? Perhaps when they had rushed into a wedding because of a child. 'Matthieu, no one has a *right* to my body except me. But I have, and *do* willingly choose to share my body with you.'

'Your body, yes. Perhaps. But…*you*?'

She bit the inside of her cheek and nodded. He wanted to know why she was so upset about seeing Sebastian.

The last time she had seen her brother was at Theo and Sofia's wedding. In the short space of time since the night of the charity gala in Iondorra and the wedding between Princess Sofia and Theo, Maria had realised quite a number of things about herself, some of them harsh and hard to bear, and others more…empowering. The determination to focus on herself had been in some ways both wondrous and liberating. Until she had discovered she was pregnant and suddenly the thought of facing Sebastian with the consequences of her reckless actions had felt awfully like a betrayal.

'My brother has always looked out for me. Been there for me when…when it became clear that my father was not going to be.' Maria sighed, hating how the well of emotion catching at the back of her throat shuddered through her breath. 'After my mother died, my father just…he seemed to give up on everything. He went through the motions for a few years, marrying Valeria, seeking one failed business deal after another, but as I got older he seemed to look at me differently. Seeing not me, but my mother looking back at him. I could tell how painful it was for him, how it was tearing at him. I don't know which one of us started it first, but each in our own ways began to avoid each other, to ease the constant hurt that hovered between us when we met.'

Maria shivered at the memories from her childhood, hiding in various rooms within the house when she knew her father was home. She'd spent hours staring at the pictures in the family photo albums, obsessively consuming the images of the mother she had never known. Each time, Seb would come and find her. Take her out into the garden, try to distract her. Even then, all those years ago Seb had protected her.

'When my father lost nearly everything in one last investment deal, I was about eight years old. Seb was barely eighteen and was forced to act—or we would have been declared bankrupt. He took over the decision-making, finding ways to save what little was left of the family's finances. Everything was sold. Our home, estates, almost all the belongings in the houses, paintings, antiques and antiquities, all just enough to pay off the millions owed because of my father's stupidity and negligence. The shame my father had brought on the Rohan de Luen name and title was enough to get us exiled from Spain.'

Across the years, Maria could hear the echoes of the arguments, the bitter accusations, Valeria's tears and recriminations, and through it all was the almost deadly determination of her brother. To be the man her father couldn't be, the protector, the decision-maker...

'What Seb did at the age of eighteen was incredible. He moved us to Italy, found a school for me, started a hotel business from the one property we had left in Europe, which managed to provide enough to keep Valeria and my father if not happy, then at least within some semblance of the life they were accustomed to. But they lived elsewhere. So it was just us. An eighteen-year-old looking after an eight-year-old.'

And only now that she was pregnant with her own child did Maria truly realise what a sacrifice her brother had made. She had known, previously, what he had given up for her. The decisions and sacrifices he had made had all revolved around her needs. And Maria had never really felt worthy of it. Any of it. She had, instead, felt more of a burden. And that ache in her heart had never really gone away.

'So your father was never really there?'

'For a while he tried. Seemed to make some kind of an effort, at least that's what I thought, until my sixteenth birthday.' Maria shivered. She hated thinking of that day, let alone actually talking of it. She had never shared that day, her feelings from it, with anyone. Fearful of the two possible reactions. That she would either be told to get over it, or they would understand... and the understanding? That would make it worse, because that would mean that the sadness, the anger, the pain...were justified. And that justification would be absolutely the worst. Because it meant that her father really didn't care…and that there was no hope for a future reconciliation.

'Seb had arranged everything. He would return from Rio where he was doing his latest business deal and for once, the family would come together. We would go to my favourite restaurant in Siena—right by the Palazzo Pubblico—long after the tourists had gone back to their hotels. I wanted to look grown up, to look beautiful… It was my sixteenth and I was about to become a woman and my family would be there to celebrate with me. Just for once it would be about me, not Valeria, not my father, not even my mother. But me.'

Goosebumps had risen on her arms as her memories took her back to that night. She almost smiled at the way she had got ready that evening. She'd forgotten how excited she'd been that night. How she had spent an hour tackling her eye make-up, getting her eyeliner *just right*. How she had admired herself in the mirror, the dress she had chosen especially for that day, the v neckline revealing the beautiful sliver threads of her mother's necklace, the way the waistline nipped in and then flared out at her hips. She felt…so grown up.

'What happened?' Matthieu asked gently, clearly aware that the ending to the tale was not a happy one.

Maria cast a glance to the night sky descending over the placid lake, the colours oddly reminiscent of the sky over Siena that evening.

'Seb had sent a car for me. It took me to the restaurant where I would meet everyone. When the chauffeur opened the car door for me, I felt like a movie star.' She laughed. 'Everyone was looking at the beautiful girl being escorted to a table in one of Siena's finest restaurants. And when I got to the table and saw that I was the first to arrive, that was okay. I could handle that. I was a grown up that night,' Maria said with the same false bravado she had felt in that instant. That even though her heart had dropped, and fear had begun to creep in, she had kept that smile on her face and even ordered a glass of champagne. Because they would come. They would be there, they just needed a little more time.

'People stopped staring after a few minutes, but as the time dragged on, as ten minutes turned to twenty and then thirty, curiosity won out and they resumed their watchful gaze on the girl who sat alone at a table for four. I hadn't really made many friends at school, so it was supposed to be just us. My family.

'Almost an hour later—' she shook her head at the memory, the first genuine smile gracing her mouth '—*he* came.'

'Your father?'

'No.'

'Sebastian?'

'Nope,' she said again, shaking her head. 'Theo Tersi. He explained that he was a friend of Seb's and that my brother's flight had been delayed because of bad weather and that he'd asked Theo to come and let me know as he'd been in the area meeting with a local vintner. Theo must have seen, must have realised in an instant that my father wasn't coming, but said nothing.

Instead, he sent all the waiters in the restaurant into a panic as he demanded the most exquisite, the most expensive things on the menu, because—he announced loudly and proudly—it was "this beautiful woman's birthday".'

Tears gathered even now at the memory of Theo's kindness that night. She had never forgotten it and, in turn, it had shaped so much of the following years of her life.

'When I got home, Theo parked his car beside Seb's and I rushed into the house to see him, so pleased that he was home. I heard him before I saw him. He was on the phone with our father.'

She had crept up to the office where Seb was, the light from the room dimly illuminating the corridor through the partially open door.

What do you mean, you were busy? It's your daughter's birthday, for God's sake... I don't care about your excuses. Enough is enough. This will never happen again, do you hear me? Otherwise I will stop providing the finances for your and Valeria's lifestyle. I will cut ties. Do you understand?'

'My father was present the following year for my birthday, but not because he wanted to be there, but because my brother had threatened to stop his finances. After that...' Maria shrugged '... I didn't really like celebrating my birthday.'

Because what she couldn't tell him, what she could barely admit to herself, was the fact that on her sixteenth birthday it had felt like a rejection of her, of who she was becoming. And she had never wanted to put herself, her *sense* of self, on the line like that again.

Silence fell between them, a silence full of sorrow and ache, of compassion—which she could see shining in Matthieu's eyes—one that hurt almost as much as the memories of that night.

'I'm sorry that the two people who were most important to you couldn't have been there that night.'

Her heart juddered in her chest, as if both soothed and ripped open at the same time.

'After that Seb became almost consumed with being there for me. Being the father that our own could not. He looked out for me, paid for my education, my travels, anything I could ever want for. In some ways he stopped being my brother. And every gift, every penny he gave me, it felt…dutiful and tainted at the same time. As if it wasn't for me, but almost in spite of our father. And as such… I just wanted to be me. I wanted to be independent, to fund myself, to… I don't know. I could never repay my brother financially, but I wanted so much to show him that I was worthy of his investment, that I wasn't a screw-up.'

'Is that how you see yourself?'

'Pregnant and in a marriage for the sake of my child?' She smiled sadly. 'I just wanted not to need him, not rely on him in any way so that we could go back to just being brother and sister…'

So that I be loved by him because he can, not because he has to.

But looking deep into her husband's eyes, she wondered whether she was still thinking of her brother.

'Maria,' Matthieu said, taking her hand in his. 'I cannot make promises that I will always be there—'

'You're working a *force majeure* into a promise?'

Matthieu laughed, sudden and joyful, breaking some of the weight of the moment and bringing a smile to her lips.

'What does my wife know of contract clauses?'

'My brother is a leading international business figure. He calls it the Act of God clause, in case unforeseeable events prevent a contract being fulfilled.'

'Act of God. Okay, I can go with that,' Matthieu said, firming his grip on her hand.

'*Force majeure* aside, I will do everything in my power that you should never feel such a thing again.'

As Matthieu said the words, he felt them slip deep within him and take hold. He looked at the woman sitting across from him, the pain in her eyes almost too much to bear. His family might have been taken from him at a very young age, but he had never doubted their love for him. Not once. Yet here Maria sat, unsure of love from the two people that should have loved her the most. And he hoped upon hope that he had just made a promise that he could fulfil.

He understood her need for independence, that sense of self he'd admired from the first moment he'd met her and, even more so, when she'd brushed aside the accusations she was simply after his money when she had come to tell him about their child. He could see that she hated that she was now reliant on *him*.

'Maria, whether it's clothes, a lifestyle that you think is not yours, but provided for you by me, it's not. What is mine is yours. I meant that the day I said "I do". No matter what. That doesn't take away from you, who you are or what you've achieved. I'd like to think that you could see that it is only something that adds.'

She exhaled a long and low breath. One he wasn't sure how to interpret. Until her eyes narrowed and transformed, an impish light breaking the seriousness of the conversation. 'And now I'm hungry. And not for food. So, husband, are you going to make good on your promise and allow me my feast?'

He refused to withhold the smile he felt pulling at his lips. Refused to turn away from the warmth blooming within his chest. It was more than carnal desire, it was something like happiness. And if this was what it was like to live with the leash lifted ever so lightly, he wanted more. He wanted to know what life was lived like, not in the shadows of his grief, but in the light of Maria.

CHAPTER NINE

As MARIA EXITED the car that had picked her and Matthieu up from the private airfield just outside Siena she clung to the words he had given her two nights before. Promises that she was not less than she had been for getting unexpectedly pregnant and marrying him, that he would be there for her. Always. *No matter what*.

She wasn't naïve enough to expect that her father might be here today, she wasn't really sure that he even knew that she was pregnant and married, and she couldn't quite bring herself to care. She had long ago given up on being concerned about his thoughts and feelings towards her. But Seb? Her brother? He had given her so much…and somehow she wanted to pay that back by being worthy…or by somehow being someone he could be proud of.

She pressed down the soft silks of the beautiful dress Matthieu had surprised her with yesterday as the wind blew about her and soothed both her nerves and her restless child.

'Are you okay?' Matthieu asked as he came around the car to stand beside her.

Maria nodded. 'I think our child is looking forward to meeting their uncle,' she said with a smile and another sweep of the now very much unavoidable bump she carried before her. 'Are *you* okay?' she said, thinking of the quiet that had almost consumed him throughout their journey.

He looked confused. 'Why would I not be?'

'Sebastian can be a little overprotective. He is, after all, my brother.'

He shrugged a shoulder. 'I have tackled multibillion-dollar deals with the world's toughest CEOs. Your brother will not be a problem.'

'If you say so,' Maria responded, a little sceptical at how dismissive Matthieu was of her concern. Perhaps she had misunderstood the reason for his brooding.

The door swung open and there he stood in the middle of three arched domes in the centre of the estate's façade. It was Sebastian's most cherished holding. It had been one of the first purchases he'd made once he had secured all the Rohan de Luens' finances. It was beautiful, perfectly formed. Not obscene as some of the estates Maria remembered from Spain, but large and nestled amongst a modest ten hectares of land, with some old and mostly untouched vineyards that Theo had always itched to get his hands on.

Seb had refused all of his entreaties, enjoying instead the wildness and untouched way it had sprawled beyond the broken, aged wooden confines and grew rampant and wild. In part, Maria liked to think that he kept it that way because it had inspired one of the first pieces of jewellery she had created.

Unconsciously she sought out Matthieu's hand and suddenly Maria was struck by how important it was for Seb to like her husband. Not the dark stranger she had met all those months ago, but the man she had come to know and like, the man that she was beginning to see he could be. Her inner voice scoffed at the soft word used to describe the complex emotion that had begun to form around her feelings for Matthieu.

But before her mind could follow that thought, Matthieu had started to walk forward and they were quickly face to face with Sebastian, whose eyes had rested on her very visible bump and had widened with something like…awe. And even he, though she could tell he was struggling to hold it back, couldn't prevent the smile from forming at his lips.

Any words in her mind were cut off as he dragged her into an embrace so powerful and consuming she felt a little as if she were coming home.

When he was done, instead of returning her to where she had stood, he placed her beside him, almost putting himself between her and Matthieu.

Her brother looked Matthieu up and down, and Maria was a little surprised that Matthieu let him, given the challenge that was locked into Sebastian's gaze. After a moment, as if Matthieu had allowed her brother his fill, he thrust out a hand and introduced himself. It was a beat before her brother accepted his hand. She rolled her eyes.

And so it begins.

'Come,' Seb said, apparently deciding that he needn't introduce himself in some form of alpha power play. 'The others are already here.'

'Others?' Maria hissed, trying to keep her voice away from Matthieu's keen hearing.

'Theo and Sofia were in the area,' he said, brushing her concern aside.

'You called in back up?' Maria demanded.

'Why would I need back up?' he replied.

Matthieu hadn't missed the way Sebastian had specifically positioned Maria out of his reach. Divide and conquer was a worthy route to take when being introduced to the husband of your sister, he supposed. He didn't have a sister, never had, but would like to think that he would be as ferociously protective of her as Seb appeared to be. He didn't have to like it, but he could most definitely respect it. Furthermore, while he *could* respect it, it didn't necessarily mean he would roll over and expose whatever soft belly Sebastian might be fool enough to think he had.

As he followed Maria and her brother down a corridor of terracotta Matthieu fought to shake off the tendrils of the nightmare he'd had the previous evening. The first one he'd had in years. He'd tried to dismiss it as mental foolishness, but it had sunk its claws into his heart and kept him almost silent on the way to Siena. He doubted very much it had anything to do with meeting Maria's brother, but couldn't shake the thought that it might have something to do with his feelings for his wife.

They rounded a corner and entered a large and surprisingly beautiful living area, bringing Matthieu back to the present. The soft cream and burnt-orange colours surprisingly soothing to a man who lived in monochrome. Instantly Matthieu eyed the presence of another man and his wife, who for a second were mid-conversation. The tall, dark-haired man Matthieu realised must have been Theo Tersi, and the woman, the Crown Princess of Iondorra.

For a second, Theo turned and cast him such a fierce look, Matthieu was impressed. Until the princess took one look at Maria and descended into squeals of pure delight and hand-wringing, which completely cut the tension in the room.

'Maria! Look at you,' the princess cried, rushing up from her seat and taking Maria in her arms, leaning back slightly as if not to crush the baby. 'Can I?' she asked, and, barely giving Maria a second to answer, her hands swept around the swell of their child. 'Oh, you are positively blooming.' And then she covered her hand with her mouth. 'Oh, that's such a trite thing to say, but you are!'

Maria laughed, the men in the room rolled their eyes, and the princess laughed again.

'Matthieu,' Maria said, turning to him, 'this is Princess Sofia de Loria of—'

'Please. No titles here. We're family.' The exquisite petite blonde woman turned to Matthieu and struck him with an aquamarine gaze.

Matthieu had met with more royals than he could shake a stick at and, no matter her pleas for familiarity, still bowed his head ceremoniously.

'Your Highness.'

Sofia laughingly sighed. 'Okay, but it's Sofia from here on out.' She turned to Maria. 'Now, we're just going to let the men do their thing and once they've got their chest-beating out of their system, we can eat,' and the princess drew Maria from the room, while his wife cast worried looks at each of the three men.

For a moment, they watched the retreating forms of the two women, and then returned their attention to each other. Finally deciding to get this over with, Matthieu gestured for them to continue, to which Sebastian simply raised an eyebrow and Theo simply sighed.

'So, Montcour—'

'It's perhaps a little late to be asking about my intentions,' Matthieu cut in. He might be respectful of Sebastian's position, but that didn't change a lifetime of being in control and in charge.

'And there I was, going to ask you if you wanted a drink. But that's fine,' Sebastian replied with an insincere shoulder shrug. 'We can get straight to business. Your reputation, whilst discreet, is colourful.'

'And yours, while quite shockingly public, is perhaps a little obvious,' Matthieu shot back. Before coming here, he had most definitely done his research.

'Obvious?' Seb said, as if outraged.

Theo made a face to suggest that there might have been something in what Matthieu was implying.

Seb must have caught it. 'I don't know what you're so smug about, *TT*.'

Theo simply grinned back at his friend.

'I think we can all agree that our reputations *before* have little bearing on *now*,' Matthieu said.

'Absolutely not. You have married my sister!'

'Yes.'

'And she's pregnant!'

'Yes,' Matthieu said again, his tone almost bored. 'These are undeniable facts.'

Sebastian scowled. 'I take it there wasn't a pre-nup, given the hastiness of the wedding that ensured Maria's family and friends would not attend.'

'That was Maria's decision,' he replied, refusing to allow the sting of guilt and the righteousness of Sebastian's ire to penetrate his thoughts.

'The pre-nup or the wedding guests?'

Sidestepping the answer, Matthieu pressed on. 'Maria is entitled to everything I have.'

'Everything?' Theo queried.

Matthieu shrugged. 'All seven point four billion dollars of it, should she want it.'

Even Sebastian looked begrudgingly impressed.

'Is it in writing?' he demanded.

'It is with my lawyers.'

Seb glanced at Theo, who shrugged.

'For Maria, it's not about money.'

'Yes,' Matthieu agreed. 'I've realised that.'

'Her life, her childhood, it wasn't easy.' Sebastian bit out the words through a jaw so clenched Matthieu feared for his dentist. 'I... I tried to provide what her—our—father was unable to. Montcour—she is exclusively the *only* thing in this world I care for. And if you hurt her, I swear to God—'

'You will be entitled to take whatever form of revenge you deem fit,' Matthieu said easily and sincerely. 'Truly.'

Sebastian narrowed his eyes as if trying to work out what Matthieu's game was.

'I mean it.'

He cocked his head to one side. 'Maria may come across as spirited and independent, but there is a softness to her that people like us can so easily crush.' Matthieu frowned at the description, an action that Seb caught. 'You disagree?'

'When I think of Maria I don't see softness, I see strength. Determination. She is fierce when challenged and quick with her laughter and her generosity. She is truly unique and very much a credit to the Rohan de Luen name.'

'Don't think to win me over with compliments, Montcour.'

'I have neither the inclination nor the desire to do so,' Matthieu pressed on. 'No offence, but you matter very little to me. All that does is Maria. She clearly wants the two—*three*,' he said acknowledging the importance of Theo in her family unit, 'of us to get on. I'm sure that we can manage to be civil.'

'There will be nothing civil about me if you break her heart,' Sebastian warned.

'As I said. That I understand and respect. I'd expect nothing less from my wife's brother.'

A gentle knock interrupted the conversation. Sofia stepped over the threshold.

'Lunch will be about twenty minutes, and, Matthieu, you can find Maria in the room on the second floor, third door on the left. I believe that you've all had enough *manticulating* for now. If not, then perhaps it could resume after dessert?'

Matthieu couldn't help but smile at the sweetly intoned speech Sofia had just delivered and, casting a last look at Sebastian and Theo, went in search of Maria.

Maria was in the room she stayed in when visiting with Sebastian. The last time she'd been here was nearly a year ago celebrating the end of her degree, which… now felt like a lifetime ago. So much had happened since then, she couldn't help but think as she smoothed a hand over a belly that contained a child. *Their* child.

The room was large, soft and warm, but oddly she found herself comparing it to the stark but beautiful estate on the edge of Lake Lucerne. Maria had lived in many places over the years, always reluctant to see any of them as a home, after their exile from Spain, but that was exactly how she'd begun to see Matthieu's estate. *Her home.*

Over by the far wall were the ten boxes she'd shipped here before she went to marry Matthieu. And oddly she found herself half hesitant, half urgent, to riffle through her jewellery equipment and materials.

She was just about to cross the room when she heard a knock on the door. Turning, she called for Matthieu to enter. She knew it was him, felt it on her skin, in the air, as if somehow she had become so attuned to his presence, she just…knew.

'Hi,' he said as he stepped into the room, taking it all in with one expansive gaze, before finally settling back on her. It gave her the time to assess for any physical damage.

'So it didn't descend into fisticuffs, then?' she asked, half afraid of the answer.

'Why would it have? I *can* be charming, you know.'

'It wasn't you I was worried about.'

'They are both perfectly intact, I assure you.'

Maria couldn't help but smile, only to follow the return of his gaze to the boxes lining the far wall. She turned back to look at them too. The sum total of her life in London.

'What are in those boxes?'

'Mostly equipment and materials.'

'You sent them here?'

Rather than bring them with you?

The implied question rang in the air like the vibrations of a bell tolled.

She walked over to one of the boxes and peeked into the depths where the tape had come away. She couldn't help but smile as she peeled back the tape a little more and slipped her hand inside to retrieve the spool of silver threading. She ran her hand over it, caressing it like a long-lost friend. Only now did she realise how much she had missed her time in the studio space she had rented in Bermondsey. The busy hum of others as they worked around her, each person lost in their own imagination, bent on creating reality from dreams.

'I didn't want to look as if I was moving in and taking over,' she replied, the lie falling heavily even to her own ears.

She felt Matthieu move across the room behind her, the heat from his body warming the cool that had descended over her. Using that heat, feeding off it, she went to the small lock box of finished pieces that she had packed shortly after returning to London after their first meeting in Switzerland when she had told him about their baby.

Opening it, she removed one of the pieces from the clear plastic bag and unwrapped the soft tissue paper carefully protecting it. It was a ring—the last piece she had made before discovering she was pregnant. This was the first piece she had made since the exhibition that wasn't a commission. That wasn't for someone else. This one had been for her.

'It's beautiful,' Matthieu said quietly and with some reverence.

'Thank you.' Pride gently shimmered through her words. A small pearl sat within a swirl of beaten gold, sweeping up around the orb like a wave, as if on the brink of concealing the beautiful natural formation. She had always been fascinated by the concentric layering of pearls… How something so stunning was formed through layers and layers of calcium carbonate surrounding what was once an irritant to the small mollusc that created it. This pearl hadn't been considered perfect enough to be classed as a gemstone, but it was no less precious to her.

'Do you miss it?'

'Yes and no,' she replied honestly. 'Coming home from Iondorra, after… Theo and Sofia, after you… I was determined to forge a "new me",' she said slightly ironically. 'To put aside the childish fantasies I had hidden behind for years. That night…it was so much for me,' she said, turning back to Matthieu. 'I realised so many things. Like how I'd been hiding behind an infatuation with an idea of someone, when in truth the reality of you was so…overwhelming. And how much I had allowed my brother to protect me from the harsh realities of life. And while that was fine, it felt as if I'd also been protected from other experiences.

'Before I discovered I was pregnant, I threw myself into a lot of commissioned work—many of which had come from my first exhibition. I was almost feverish in the determination to make this "work" pay, to provide security for myself, to become independent from Sebastian, from anyone really.'

She paused, now thinking of the way her imagination had unfurled in the last few months. The way that her self-imposed hiatus from jewellery had, in a way, fed her starved creativity, which had diminished since she'd accepted more commissions after her show.

'Thinking of it now, I was running before I could walk. I was overwhelmed by how wonderful it was that people wanted my work, but somehow sacrificed some of my *self* in the process. I think I lost a little of that— was certainly at risk of morphing into the extreme of what I had always wanted.'

'And what was that?'

'I just wanted enough. Enough to get by and allow me the time and finances to pursue the pieces that I *really* wanted to make. And if people, customers, wanted those pieces, all the better. But I never wanted to lose the love of it—I never wanted to destroy the one thing that had given me so much pleasure and so much… company during my childhood.'

'Company?'

'Sorry, that sounds strange. But even as a child, I would spend hours lost in my imagination, designing pieces in my mind, trying to work out how it could be done, what materials would be best…'

'You were lonely?'

'A little perhaps. Seb was forced to work all hours to ensure that the family didn't lose *everything*. My father and Valeria were rarely there, either locked away in a different part of Italy, or still desperately trying to cling to a lifestyle they no longer had. Meanwhile I had been thrust into a new school with a new language, which didn't exactly form the best basis for deep and lasting friendships.'

Matthieu seemed to take that in before turning back to the ring. 'May I?'

Maria gently pressed it into his open hand.

'So without commissions, this is what you like to create?'

'Yes.' The smile returning to her lips warmed the word, warmed her deep within.

'There is space in Lucerne for a studio if you—'

'No,' Maria interrupted. 'No, that is a kind offer, but… I prefer to be around others when I work. There's a strange but wonderful feeling when you are lost in your own world, yet surrounded by others. It feels…'

'Less lonely?'

Matthieu silently cursed. He couldn't help but think that he had somehow taken this bright and beautiful woman and hidden her away from the world. Dragged her back to his lair, and for a moment he feared that he might actually be harming her. Keeping her locked away from the sunlight and from the things that she needed most.

He cursed the nightmare that had somehow lifted the lid on memories he had not confronted for years. Because he knew so well, too well, how lonely a child could be. All those days, weeks and months spent in a hospital room, checked on by nurses and visited by Malcolm, but when he was alone, the silence had wrapped around him and become deafening.

A silence that had carried on in his life until… Until Maria.

Matthieu bit back another curse. Even as Maria spoke of the need for company, to be surrounded by people and life, all he wanted to do was take her back to Lucerne and surround her with himself. To protect her, hide her away from the world where she only knew him. The beast began to stir in his breast again, roaring *mine*. As if his heart had recognised her as his and only his, the world outside be damned.

And that, above all things, scared him the most. Because he had worked so hard, for so many years, to ensure that he was never bound in such a way to another person. And now that he was…

Matthieu pushed aside the thought that had grown thorns and threatened to bloom into his mind. He looked at Maria, lost in her own thoughts as she caressed the spun silver in her hands, and purposefully unfurled his clenched hand to reveal the ring she had made before she had come to live with him.

'It doesn't have to be that way any more, Maria,' he said, no longer sure if he was talking about her loneliness or his past.

'It doesn't feel as if it is,' she said, her hand once again sweeping over the outline of their child. Her eyes held a ring of truth, shining within them, offering, rather than asking for, assurance. An assurance he suddenly wanted to turn from. Because his wife was upsetting everything he thought about his life. Every natural instinct to turn around and retreat, to close himself off from the world just as he was beginning to

hope. To hope for something more than the constraints
he'd put on his heart the night of the fire.

'You can stay, Maria, if you need—or want,' Sebastian
said, sweeping her up in his arms to say goodbye even
as his words contradicted his actions. She smiled, relishing the comfort and more that her brother offered.

The meal had been delicious—Matthieu keeping
to his promise to eat everything she chose for herself,
making her smile and the men at the table sceptical. Although the conversation had been a little slow to start,
Sofia and Maria making the most of it, both her husband and her brother had soon relaxed into the gentle,
teasing tone that had descended. And it had felt glorious to Maria, who had been so worried at the thought
of any kind of confrontation. She had been so grateful
to Sofia, who had completely put aside her faux pas
from the night of the gala in Iondorra, and now when
Maria looked at Theo she marvelled at how deeply
wrongly she had interpreted not only their relationship but her own feelings for him. Joy rose within her
chest as she thought now of how they had found happiness together...the same kind of happiness she had
found with Matthieu perhaps? She couldn't help but
cast her mind into a future where she and her husband
surrounded a beautiful child, with dark wayward curls
and devastating honey-green eyes, with love and happiness. Some long-distant sunlit future, the thought of
which filled her with inescapable joy.

'That's okay. I'm good, really, Seb. I am.' And

she felt it too. Somehow talking to Matthieu, sharing something of herself with him had forged a connection deep within her. Unaccountably she felt overwhelmed by emotion. As if being reunited with her things had triggered something—and not just the idea that had sparked in her mind the moment she'd seen her equipment and materials. The urge to create something for Matthieu, something that would potentially mean so much to him. She couldn't shake the feeling that she wanted to give something back to him. Because in a way, that was what he had done for her. Bringing her here, to see her brother, to stand beside her. She had shrugged into the safety he had offered her. The future.

One where she realised that now she *could* make the jewellery that she wanted to. Not dependent on commissions, not dependent on her meagre pay cheque from the café. And she wondered at how different it felt. Accepting the financial security he offered, when everything in her had railed against the same from her brother.

Trust. She felt it unfurl within her. She was beginning to trust him. Trust that he would be there for her and her child. And it began to fill her, consume her and make her feel… Excited for what was to come? Hopeful?

Seb released her from his hold, casting a glance over her shoulder to where Matthieu was arranging for all the boxes from her room to be sent on to the private jet waiting to take them back to Switzerland. *'Mi amor,'* he said and sighed. 'I am pleased for you.

And for this little one,' he said, his eyes crinkling and his hand warm on her belly. 'And I suppose Montcour is acceptable,' he begrudgingly admitted. 'But… I do know of his childhood. I know what happened to him, and that kind of damage, that kind of baggage… Anyone would have to be blind not to see how closely he guards his heart. I just fear that those walls might be a little too high even for you to climb.'

'We all have baggage, Sebastian.'

'Perhaps, but I just want you to take care.'

As Maria and Matthieu were whisked away from Seb's estate in Siena and towards the small private airfield, she tucked away her brother's warning. Put it into a box and buried it deep. Because for the first time in what felt like for ever, she wanted to hold onto this feeling. To keep it within her and let it warm her from the inside out. Let it nurture both her and her child. Because this feeling, Maria realised, was love.

CHAPTER TEN

A SILENT SCREAM tore from Matthieu's mouth as he bolted up from the bed. He was covered in that kind of cold unnatural sweat that came from a night terror. The kind that he'd experienced three times already in the weeks since returning from Siena with Maria.

Heart pounding in his chest and shivering, he turned to where Maria lay on her side in the bed, the only balm to his soul that she hadn't been woken by his nightmare. He rubbed a hand over his face to try and erase the memories of the haunting dream. The way his father had looked at him from the window of their home, flames licking around the edges of the wooden frame, the crackling, screaming sound that filled his ears as the fire consumed everything in its path.

Even now his gut churned, his heart twisted just like the flames in his imagination…because it wasn't a dream. It was a memory. Or had been until he'd seen Maria over his father's shoulders, looking down at him as she caressed her heavily pregnant bump, seemingly unaware of the danger she was in. She had looked at him with trust, with complete acceptance, as if she truly believed that he, in the body of an eleven-year-old, would find a way to save her.

In the dream he had screamed until his throat was raw and, now awake, it felt scratched, thick with an ache that wouldn't quit. Casting one last look at his wife, serene in her peaceful sleep, he peeled back the damp sheets and padded from the room, each step rippling beneath the icicles that covered his back and chest.

He turned on the shower, not seeing past the images that had haunted his nights and even sometimes during his days, during moments of weakness that he had come to hate as much as his memories. It had been fifteen years since he'd last had these dreams, since he'd built up his mental and emotional defences to protect himself from them.

And now they were back. Because of Maria. Because of his wife.

Because on the brink of fatherhood himself, he could no longer understand the actions of his father. Or worse…because for the first time in his life, he actually did. He did understand why his father chose to seek out his wife that night, rather than finding his own freedom, rather than choosing his son. He understood the sheer magnitude of what tied his father to his mother, and him to Maria.

Matthieu's legs buckled in the shower, as if he'd been sucker punched low in his belly and every single thing in him hurt, ached, cried out for…the devil knew what. He stifled the cry that raged and thrashed within his chest, furious for release, desperate to be heard. He thrust his fisted hand, white knuckled, into his mouth and bit down to prevent its escape.

Nausea swirled in his stomach and he tried to suck in lungsful of air around the streaming water, around the hand in his mouth. He hadn't had a panic attack for years and he knew what he should do, but was helpless against the thick clogging fear that had descended over his mind.

The sound of his heartbeat mixed with the pounding of the water's jets from the shower head and all he wanted to do was curl up on the smooth white flooring beneath him. But something, somewhere deep within him, prevented it. A sign of weakness that even in his darkest moment he refused to succumb to.

He had no idea of how long he had stayed like that but finally, and only when the pain in his muscles cut through his lost thoughts, he reached up to turn off the water. As he towelled himself off, choosing not to return to his bed, *their* bed, he stalked the corridors of his home and sought out the gym, even though every instinct in him wanted to go back to Maria. Instead he turned to the treadmill, exhausting himself further until he might eventually fall back into a dreamless sleep where nothing and no one could reach him.

Maria stretched an arm out to Matthieu's side of the bed and frowned at once again finding it empty. She had tried to ask him about it after the first night, but he had brushed aside her concerns and insisted that he was fine. That he was distracted by an issue with one of the mining companies. The next time his absence was explained by a midnight international phone call. And Maria honestly couldn't remember the following reasons.

In the deep reaches of her heart, she knew he was pulling away. Could feel him almost imperceptibly slipping through her fingers, even as her love for him made her grip tighter, hold on as hard as she could. As if it was the only thing that would keep him with her. So she half believed his excuses and instead focused on making the spark of an idea she'd had back in Siena a reality.

She had sought out a studio in Lucerne, not too far from their home, and the moment Matthieu left for work, she would leave herself. She would share a conspiratorial smile with the driver she had sworn to secrecy and pass the ride to the studio with images of Matthieu's happy surprise when she presented her gift to him. She was sure, so sure, that he would be filled with joy when he saw what she had created for him.

Days before she had sneaked into his bedroom and retrieved the small box hidden in a drawer of the side cabinet. Opening the badly burned box had revealed a thick, broad silver ring, blackened by fire and partially melted. Her heart had ached for the small boy who had lost everything but this. Ached for the man who felt that he had to hide it away, rarely to be looked at or acknowledged. Remembering how happy he had been for her that she had her mother's necklace, something she could have with her every day, had given her the confidence that she was right in her plans for him to have the same. She had taken it from its allotted space and wrapped it as carefully as she imagined she would one day swaddle their child. From that moment in her room in Siena she had been consumed with need to give Matthieu something of his past that he could keep with him at all times. Something that he could cherish. The moment she laid eyes on it, she saw how she could clean the dirt and damage from the precious metal and had seen what she could do with it. How she could re-forge the symbol of his grief into something new. She would use the silver of the ring to form the basis of a new piece, a new creation, from both past and present that he could carry with him into his future.

Still a little concerned about the impact of the fumes on her unborn child, she had instead focused on the mould for the piece she wanted to create. For hours she would lose herself in the design, carefully choosing how much additional silver would be needed to create the bracelet she wanted to give him, where to place it in order to retain the purity of precious metal belonging to the ring and how to join the two representations of the past and present. For hours she would lose herself in the shaping of the mould, pouring her love for Matthieu, for their unborn child, layering every single ounce of it she had, into the work that became almost her sole focus. Because even though she would deny it to herself, deep down she couldn't help but feel that time was running out for her. For them.

She had met with Georges Sennate and had immediately found a kindred spirit. The owner of the small studio was perhaps nearing seventy, even though his eyes twinkled like those of a teenager. She had come to relish his owl-like stare as he'd opened his space to her, shared the excitement of the piece she was creating for her husband. And had been touched as he'd offered his thoughts and knowledge of his own silverwork with her. And Maria had been so thankful that she had met someone that she could entrust such an important part of the process to. She could tell from the way that he showed as much care to her work as his own that he was the right person to melt the silver for her. Heat it to the point where the dark smoke stains could be swept aside, cleansed in the same way she had come to realise Matthieu had cleansed her, her childhood hurts slipping away with the hours she spent creating her gift to him.

She watched Georges's form bent over the forge, pouring the silver into the moulds below a large air vent from about three metres away. The heated silver glowing in the darkness like a living thing. It would set and then she'd be able to go to work. She knew that soldering would be okay, if she wore a mask to protect her, and her fingers itched to get to work on the piece she wanted to present to him at dinner in just four days' time.

She had only told Matthieu that it was a special occasion. Some strange inclination had her withholding the fact that it was her birthday. Because she didn't want that night to have the burden of history. Maria wanted to start that celebration anew with Matthieu. The new beginning she had never known she'd wanted.

Matthieu sat in his leather chair staring out of the window of his office in Zurich almost obsessively counting the minutes passing the hour he should have met Maria in the restaurant. But he couldn't move. In the last few days, Maria's simple acceptance of his withdrawal had become somehow worse than any kind of argument or demand. The beast within him wanted to rage, wanted to snarl and gnash its teeth and, although he wouldn't want to unleash that onto Maria, the fact that she accepted his behaviour caused it only to increase. He felt as if he were building to some impossible point where he would explode and his head pounded with the need of it. A combination of lack of sleep, the nightmares and his wife was almost too much to bear.

All his assurances that he would never treat her like her father, that he would be there for her, came back to haunt him as he struggled almost by the second with what he wanted and what he feared the most. Because in the last few days, his nightmare had morphed and changed into something new, something far more terrifying. He was no longer the small boy looking up at his father in the window. Now he had assumed the role of the father, looking down at his child and being torn between his wife and his son. It had played out in each and every conceivable way. Sometimes he went to his child, sometimes he went to Maria…but each and every time it hurt, sliced open his heart as he was only ever able to save one without the other.

He rubbed a hand over his face, all the while watching the minute hand jerk across the clock face and, even knowing the pain he would be causing Maria, he simply couldn't move. Instinctively, he knew. He knew that by failing to show up that evening, he would force her hand, he would hurt her so greatly that she would have to walk away. He hated himself for it, but knew that it was the only option he had…for his own sanity but, more importantly, for Maria. Because he could not tie her to this life, to him. Not without destroying the very thing that he loved about her.

Maria sat in the restaurant in Lucerne, her back straight and her head high. She could see them. The stares, the supposedly surreptitious glances her way. She could feel the curiosity from the other diners in the restaurant washing over her in waves.

The waiter approached and asked if he could get her anything and she smiled, a barely audible 'no' falling from her lips. She steeled her hand, hiding the tremors at her fingers, as she reached for the water glass and hoped that she would be able to swallow it past the clogged ache in her throat.

As she placed the glass back on the table, her gaze was drawn to the small black box she had placed on the plate opposite her. She had wanted it to be one of the first things Matthieu would see. She had wanted to watch the curiosity from his face turn to delight and, even deeper, to recognition of what she had done for him. The revelation that she had understood his pain and transformed it into something new.

Instead, in the space of his absence, the fear of a different reaction had begun to invade her imagination. One of anger, one of horror as he raged at how she should never have done such a thing, how she had no right, how she had trespassed on a hurt she had no possible way of understanding.

As the minutes had ticked across the hour, her thoughts had turned from the gift to herself, as her heart lurched between him and her. Stuck between the past and the present, what she could see around her had shimmered before her eyes and instinctively she knew that there would be no rescuer tonight. Her mind battered and bargained with itself. Just five more minutes… Just another one. He might have been caught in traffic. In a meeting. In an accident. Anything that would excuse the four unanswered calls to his mobile phone. And although she would never wish that upon him, she was desperate, reaching for an excuse. Because the reality was so much more painful to bear.

She wanted to laugh even as tears threatened to fall from her eyes. Whether he had known it was her birthday or not, he could never have been naïve enough to deny that leaving her here, in a restaurant, wearing a dress she had bought just for him, would hurt her deeply. So he knew. But he had chosen to do it anyway.

Through a haze of barely formed tears, she watched

the head waiter slip through the tables discreetly, making his way towards her. She almost wanted to throw up her hand, prevent him from telling her what she already knew. But was instead stuck still. Frozen. On the brink of a precipice as if his decree as to whether Matthieu had simply been delayed, or was unable to come, would draw her back to safety or…

'Mrs Montcour, I'm terribly sorry but your husband has sent word that he has been unavoidably detained and won't be…'

Maria didn't hear the rest of the sentence over the roaring in her ears. Unaccountably the man seemed to be waiting for some response from her, and she stared up at him in confusion. Surely Matthieu couldn't really have done this to her. Surely the man she loved wouldn't inflict such pain upon her in this way.

'I just need a minute,' she said to the head waiter, who slipped back past the tables of people staring at her like their favourite TV show.

Her hand flew to her stomach when her baby kicked out as if in sympathy with her, him, or defiance, she couldn't tell. All she knew was that she could not stand for it. Could not, would not, live like this again. Not for her child, and not for herself.

It was as if the spell that had stuck her body still had been lifted and she jerked up from the seat. The noise of the chair screeched across the subdued lull of the restaurant, drawing everyone's attention. She stood there for a moment, the barest of ones, permitting their curiosity, their pity, and silently promised herself that this would never, *never*, happen again.

She reached for the small black box from across the table and, with more poise and elegance than a queen, left the restaurant even as tears rolled down her cheeks.

When Matthieu finally arrived home that night, he was exhausted. From the lack of sleep, from the emotional warring within him as he had struggled almost violently with the need to go to her in the restaurant and the desperation to stay away from her. In a last-minute moment of blind-eyed panic, he had rushed to the restaurant—realising far too late that he had been wrong. That he shouldn't, couldn't push her away. But she had already left.

He threw his keys on the side table and stalked through the estate, desperate to find her, to beg for forgiveness. The desolation, guilt and devastation he had felt had cut him off at his knees. Entering the large living area, he stared at the three suitcases by the front door. Stared at them as if he couldn't tell whether they were real or part of his twisted imagination. Couldn't tell whether he was relieved or plunged swiftly into the deepest despair he'd ever felt.

He listened for sounds of her within the house, but it was silent. The lights were off, the whole house cold and dark, as if forecasting his future without her, without his child.

The thought ignited a primal cry within him, full of pain and anger.

A breeze reached him and he looked to the French windows that led out to the decking, seeing that they were open, and finally spying Maria's silhouetted form out there beneath the night sky. Her skin, glowing beneath the light of the moon, her glorious long dark hair flowing around her shoulders, and instantly he was plunged back to that first night. The way that her entire being had called to him like a siren.

Just the way it was doing now. And for a moment, he wished he could take it all back. He wished that, instead of hiding in his office like a coward, he'd got to the restaurant in time. That he'd met her, held her, and told her how much she meant to him. But he couldn't. Instead of going backwards, he went forwards. His feet taking him through the opening in the French windows and out onto the decking, just behind her.

The slight hitch in her breathing letting him know that she knew he was there.

Neither said a word. The silence between them vibrating with unspoken hurts and needs, as if the stars alone bore witness to a great tragedy.

'Maria, I'm so—'

'Don't. Don't you dare apologise.'

She turned then and he wished she hadn't. He could see the tear tracks on her skin, the slight redness that screamed against the shocking pallor of her cheeks. Maria was not hiding her pain as he did. No. She claimed it. Owned it, was even glorious in it. He bit back a thousand curses that would send him to hell and keep him there.

'Do you know what today is?' she asked as if she wasn't flipping the switch on the detonator for a bomb he knew, *knew*, was about to change everything. He could feel it in the air, taste it on his tongue and he desperately wanted to stop the words from falling from her lips.

Instead, he bit down and shook his head, fearing her answer as much as needing to hear it.

'It's my birthday.'

Curses rose in his mind so loud until they were screaming at him. If he had known...would he have done things differently? He was so torn, so confused, in so much pain he couldn't tell any more. All this time his nightmares had shown him losing her in the most violent painful way, and now he was making it happen in reality. Pushing her away to protect himself and he knew that made him the worst kind of beast.

A small sad smile painted her beautiful features. 'Perhaps it is fitting that we met on yours and part on mine.'

'Maria—'

'And I was the one who had a present for *you*,' she said through a half-laugh, full of sadness and loss.

It was then that he saw the small box being turned over in her small hands, the paleness of her skin in contrast to the black velvet case. He frowned, trying to make sense of the shiver of apprehension that streaked through his body. But all he wanted, all he could think of was trying to make her stay.

'I was wrong, Maria. I never should have left you in that restaurant.'

'You were. And you shouldn't have. You knew what it would do to me and you did it anyway. For the first time since I met you, you truly lived up to the reputation you have clung to.'

The knife twisted in his gut, even as she thrust out her hands to give him the gift he did not deserve, had never deserved. Without taking his eyes from her, he retrieved the box and held it. 'Maria, please—'

'Open it.'

'Don't you think we have more important things to discuss right now?'

'No,' she said, shaking her head. 'Because I think that somewhere in that gift is the heart of exactly what is going on right now.'

Frowning, he pulled back the lid of the box and everything in him stopped. It was as if the sight of the contents had not only stalled his breath, but the thoughts in his mind, the blood in his veins. It took him a moment to compute what he was seeing—what he knew he should have been seeing and instead what was actually there.

The three beaten, hand-moulded, textured strands had been woven in a plait that seemed to have no beginning and no end, and though he didn't want to, though he desperately tried to hide from what Maria had created, he could sense how she had wanted each strand to represent his mother, father and himself, and then shift and morph into her, him and their child... And it might have. If it hadn't represented something to him already. Something dark and dangerous and devastating.

'You shouldn't have done this.' Matthieu barely recognised his own voice, unable to even bring himself to look at her.

'I... I thought that this would be something beautiful for you. A way to keep something of your family with you at all times.'

He could hear the confusion, the hurt, in her voice. Perhaps even a trace of fear.

'You have no idea—'

'Of course I don't, Matthieu. Because you don't talk to me! Don't tell me what you're thinking or what you're feeling.'

'You don't want to know what I'm feeling right now,' he warned her.

'But I do, Matthieu. I do. I don't just want the bits of you you deem fit for me to see. I want everything. Not the beast, not the carefully contained husband. I want *you*.'

'You want to know *me*? You want to know what I'm feeling? What I'm feeling right now is sheer horror. Horror that you would take something so personal from me and change it into something completely different. That you would take the very reason my parents are dead—' He cut himself off mid-sentence, desperately warring with himself to grip the fine strands of silver in his hands, or hurl it from him as far as he could. And it was her fault. He never would have been standing here, sharing this with her, had she not pushed, not demanded, not *wanted*.

'Matthieu, I—'

'The way my father looked at my mother when she gave him his present that night…so full of love, so full of life. They sent me to bed before I was able to get a good look at it, promising that I could see it in the morning, but…'

He shook his head at the memories. The childish frustration that he'd been sent to bed, the desperation to see more clearly what his mother had given his father.

'I was too impatient. I sneaked from my room and found it downstairs in the dining room. My parents wasted precious time searching my room, the whole of the first floor, time that they could have used to leave the burning building had it not been for me. Had it not been for this—' He held up the bracelet to punctuate his point.

'—Or what this once was, my father could have made it out. He could have leapt from the window he pushed me out of. I remember the moment he looked at me and made his decision to go back for my mother. I remember the tears I saw in his eyes, how desperate he was to be with me and desperate he was to find her. I saw him there in the window, the words of love he sent me drowned out by the sounds of the fire raging through our home.'

'I'm sorry!' his father had yelled, the words barely reaching Matthieu staring up at him with horror and fear and pain.

'Do you know what it's like to feel responsible for your parents' deaths? To wish your father had chosen you over your mother? Can you conceive of the guilt? That you would rather your mother have died alone than be alone yourself? Or, better yet, not have rescued me at all, but taken me with them?'

His voice broke on the last word. He'd never admitted that to anyone. He'd never even said it out loud.

The silence around them vibrated with thick emotion. Her warmth was the first indication he had that she had come up behind him. That she stood so close, he could feel it.

'The fire was not your fault, Matthieu,' she said, her voice breaking over the words, as if she hurt just as much as he did just then. 'Their loss was not your fault.'

'Really? You believe that? That I'm innocent of that loss, that I'm not the beast I proved to be tonight when I left you in the restaurant *on purpose*?' he bit out, hating that his fear, that his pain was making him just as cruel as she accused him of being, but simply unable to stop. Because pushing her away was safer, for her and for him.

'Don't—'

'Don't what? Lift the veil of whatever fantasy you've woven around us? The same fantasy you wove around you and Tersi? The man you thought you loved *the day we met.*'

It was as if he had struck her. The flinch yanking her head back and the colour draining from already pale features.

.

'I don't know what you're talking about.'

Confusion and pain fell from her eyes like tears, each one landing hard and fast on his heart.

'Yes, you do. You *do* know. You find people in your life to weave impossible relationships around, because that's easier for you than to face up to the reality that not everything can be a fairy tale, not everyone can be as perfect as you really want them to be. Not your father, not your brother and damn sure not me.' And even as he said the words, he half believed them, half hoped that he was speaking the truth, because the pain he was causing her, causing himself would be somehow less, and damn him if that didn't make him a bastard. 'And what is the reason for that, Maria? You once told me you wanted to know who Maria Montcour was, but, in truth, whether you're a wife, or a mother, a sister or a daughter, you don't seem to know who *you* are. And without that, we will all be playing roles in your fantasies. Ones we never have any hope of living up to. You demand love from us, but how could we if you don't even know yourself?'

Maria let his accusation lie within her. She almost felt herself shrugging into it as if rearranging a piece of clothing over her skin. The horrifying realisation that he might be right robbing her momentarily of thought. Suddenly it was as if something within her snapped into place. As if he had thrown a mirror up to a person she vaguely knew but hardly recognised. Because he was right. It was easier to play a role within these desperately fantasised relationships. Because any rejection

she experienced wasn't a denial of *her*, it was the role
that she had assigned herself, one she could discard
and move on from.

Had she really done that? All these years…she recognised the truth of it in what her feelings had once
been for Theo. But no matter what Matthieu said, she
knew that she did love him. She could see him almost
mentally scrabbling around for anything that would
push her away, that would defend himself against his
own feelings for her. And if he was going to tear strips
from her heart to reveal some inner truth, then she
would do the same for him. If this was the last time
she would ever be able to meet him with honesty then
she would.

'Oh, how righteous you are, accusing me of not
knowing myself, of hiding in roles, but what about
you, Matthieu? What are you hiding from each time
you leave my bed?'

'I have to. I have nightmares, and they are…'

'Just dreams, Matthieu.'

'No, they're not. They are real, they are memories
for me! Each night I see my father, my mother and my
house all burn. Sometimes you are there. You and our
child. And I can't—'

She could see the pain rippling across his shoulders and down his spine. Even in the warm night air,
he looked frozen, cold to the touch even as his words
were heated and blistered with pain. Her heart broke at
the sight of it. Hating that he had hidden this from her.

'Why didn't you tell me? Why didn't you talk it

through with me? We could have faced it together, but instead you bottled it up and kept it to yourself.'

'I'm not like you. You have your brother, you have family. I am alone in this, and have been for more years than I have not been. Of course I didn't tell you. I don't tell anyone anything.'

'But I'm not just anyone,' she couldn't help but cry. 'I'm your wife. A role more real than any other. And as much as you might fight it, try to deny it and palm it off as fantasy, I love you. I do. It's overwhelming, incredible and wondrous and you won't let me share that with you, which is unspeakably sad.' The words were a call to action in her heart, rippling out through her body. She hoped above all that even now, even as she knew she must walk away, he would change his mind. Change his heart.

'But you won't let that happen for yourself,' she pressed on. 'Instead you hide your pain, hoarding it as if it's precious, as if it's the only thing your parents left you with. Ignoring the fact that they gave you the building blocks to become the amazing man you could be, if you just let yourself.' She could see the way he flinched at her words as they struck home, as they knocked aside the lies he had built around his heart to protect himself. 'When I first told you about our child, you asked me what it is that I wanted. Now I'm asking you. What is it you want?'

'I don't know!' The shout left his mouth and crashed against her in the most painful way. Because she wanted to give him the benefit of the doubt, desperately wanted to help him find his way to the truth. But she couldn't.

'That's not good enough.'

'It was at the beginning. I told you that I would be there for the child. I told you that you could have whatever material thing you could ever want or need. And I told you that I could not give you more than that. You're changing the terms of our agreement.'

'Yes,' she said defiantly. 'I am changing the terms. Because you've shown me that you are capable of more than you pretended to be. And you made me want that person, you made me want more.'

Matthieu couldn't even deny it. Because he had changed. From the first moment that he saw her by the lake in Iondorra, he had known it would happen. It had started long before the nightmares that plunged him back into memories that he had long ago buried, never wanting to feel the pain, the devastation, the loss—the loss he feared he would experience if she or their child ever... He couldn't even bring himself to think it. She *had* made him want more, want to be more. But it was too much. And the beast within him ached, snarling, biting, growling and gnashing its teeth.

'And until you are ready to be the man I know you can be, I don't want to see you. I don't want you near me. You will have access to our child any time you like. I would not deny our child or you that right. But know this. When it comes to our child, there is no *force majeure*. You will be there at every birthday, every Christmas, every celebration whether it be a music exam, a school exam, or a driving test.'

Maria was painting a picture of the future he would deny himself. The future he was almost forcing through his hands like sand and it was eviscerating him.

'No *force majeure* and no three strikes. Miss one, and you are out of their life for ever. Do you understand? Because what I have learned from my childhood and my time with you is that I will not inflict any kind of physical or emotional absence upon my child.'

My child. She was removing him from her life just as he had wanted before he had returned to the house, and after she had given him the present. At first it had been because he thought they would be better off without him. Now? He simply couldn't imagine how he could live with them. Them and the constant fear that he could lose them at any moment. So yes, he needed her to go.

'My child will grow up knowing they are loved, they are supported by their family. That no matter what, they come first. And they will know that because I will lead by example. So no matter how much I love you—and I do, Matthieu, so, so much—I am putting myself and my child first. But, Matthieu, for you? You have to face this. You cannot live in the shadow of the reputation you have lived down to as beast. You cannot let it rule your life.'

She walked past him, then, head held high, so beautiful it made his heart ache. But he knew it was for the best that Maria Rohan de Luen, the woman he loved too much to bear, left his life.

CHAPTER ELEVEN

YOU CANNOT LET it rule your life.

Maria's parting words had echoed within the walls of his estate, had roamed around his mind for hours and even days after she had left.

His phone calls and emails had gone unanswered. He had not been back to the office since that night. Because in truth, her words had come to consume him. In the years following the fire he had thought, in his own way, that he had dealt with the events of that night. But now Maria had shone a light on his darkest, deepest hurts and the door that she had unlocked now swung open, fully flooding him with everything.

At first he had been cowed by the loss, a loss as fresh as it had been all those years ago. But once the first flush of memories from that night passed through him, other memories emerged. A holiday they had spent in Antigua, the way his mother always dressed in bright colours, pinks, turquoises, purples and bright oranges. The way his father would gently tease his mother for her choice in unusual earrings. And it hurt. The realisation that he had pushed down all the things that had made the two of them unique, loving, sometimes even like bickering schoolchildren. And it made him want more.

A week after Maria had left, he'd called Malcolm, who had arrived at the house within hours. The concern and shared pain on his familiar features almost a balm to Matthieu's wounds. He had peppered his oldest friend with questions about how his parents had met, what they had been like, things that perhaps he would have learned in time, had they had the luxury of it. For hours they had talked, Matthieu relishing everything he had never wanted, never been able to bear, before.

Until finally Matthieu had talked about that night. Opening up his grief for someone other than Maria to see. To own his shame and guilt over his actions that night.

'I never knew,' Malcolm had said. 'If I had... Matthieu, why didn't you tell me you felt that way?'

'Admit that it was my fault?'

'But it wasn't,' Malcolm had said, pressing a hand on the wooden table as if to hold himself back from a stronger physical act. 'Matthieu, do you remember how the fire started?'

He'd frowned, knowing by heart the fire marshal's incident report he had once scoured as if it held answers. 'Faulty electrics.'

'Where?' Malcolm had prompted.

'What do you mean?'

'Where did the fire start?'

'On the second floor.'

'And where were you?'

'Downstairs in the living…'

Malcolm had levelled him with a heavy gaze. 'The fire wasn't your fault, Matthieu, and if you'd been in bed that night, and not further down in the house, then… Then you might have been one of the first casualties of that night. Your father didn't waste precious time, and even if he had, he would have done so because he loved you and wanted you to live. If he went back into the fire for your mother it was because he wanted the same for her. Your father might have survived, but the man I was lucky enough to call my closest friend in the world wouldn't have forgiven himself if he had not tried.'

He wanted you to live. He wouldn't have forgiven himself if he had not tried.

Long after Malcolm had left, Matthieu had sat gazing, unseeing, at Lake Lucerne. He had been shocked by the realisation that he had not been living. That he had not been trying. Maria had been right. He had hoarded his pain, hoarded the precious, sometimes painful, but more often incredible loving memories of his parents as if they had a portion of allotted time before running out, before disappearing from his mind. But the more he thought, the more he remembered. And the more he realised that he had made a terrible mistake forcing Maria from his life.

Nearly a month later, Matthieu stepped out of the limousine parked outside an estate in Siena, and knocked on the door, bracing himself for what was to happen.

It swung open and Sebastian Rohan de Luen took one look at him and swung. In truth, Matthieu had seen the punch coming from a mile away, but took the hit, feeling it was pretty much deserved at this point.

He cupped his jaw, rubbing at the small sting at the corner of his mouth with his thumb.

'A friend would tell you to use your words,' he said to Seb.

'Yeah? Well. I'm more about actions. I warned you. Dammit, I bloody told you—'

'I know. You were right. I deserved it and much more.'

Seb looked at him long and hard before stepping back and letting him pass through the door and into the dark living room of the estate Matthieu had last visited with Maria. That was when Matthieu noticed the glass of half-drunk whisky and empty bottle on the table. Seb had come to a halt in the middle of the room and was staring at a painting propped up on the mantelpiece above a large fireplace. It was only then that Matthieu really looked at the painting.

'Wait…is that a—?'

'Yes.'

Matthieu was struck by the image of the woman staring out at him, from one of Europe's most famous and expensive painters.

'Jesus, is that—?'

'Our mother. The resemblance is remarkable, don't you think?'

Matthieu chose not to answer, suddenly realising

just how hard it must have been for Maria's father to see the face of his wife in his child. Suddenly realising how difficult it must have been for Maria. 'That painting must be worth at least one hundred million.'

'You aren't the only billionaire in the room, Montcour.'

'Did you *buy* this?'

A pregnant pause filled the air before Sebastian reluctantly admitted that it was a long story. Matthieu looked sideways at Sebastian. 'Are you okay?' he asked, genuinely concerned.

'I don't think you're here to talk about me and my feelings, are you, Montcour?'

'No, but—'

'Don't,' Seb interrupted, slashing his hand through the air to cut off the direction of the conversation, and resumed his watchful stance over the painting.

Matthieu sighed. 'Do you know where she is?'

'Yes.'

'Are you going to tell me?'

'Only if you give me a good enough reason to,' he replied, finally turning that powerful, predatory gaze on him.

'I love her,' Matthieu said simply. He let the truth shine from his words and fill the darkness in the room. In the last few weeks he'd spent hours thinking through his feelings, his fears and the darkest parts of him. Regretting almost every second that he'd not allowed Maria to help him in this way, but knowing that in reality it was better, healthier for him to have forged this realisation himself.

'You might do. I might even believe that you do. But that doesn't mean I will give you what you want.'

Matthieu couldn't fault him for that. It took him nearly an hour to convince Sebastian to reveal where Maria was. As he returned to his car, he pulled out his phone and got his assistant to track down the telephone number for Theo Tersi. The conversation was brief and to the point and Matthieu put all thoughts of Maria's brother aside the moment Theo promised to come to Siena as soon as humanly possible. Then, with his sole focus on Maria, he put the key in the car's ignition and hit the gas.

Maria pulled into the driveway of the house she had rented in Umbria, both physically and mentally exhausted. She had visited with her father and Valeria and it had been…she shook her head at the direction of her thoughts. Difficult? Yes. Painful? A little. But better? Perhaps.

It had taken a good few weeks of soul-searching just to find the courage to face Eduardo. To be truly honest with herself. She had allowed her father's withdrawal to dictate far too much of her life. She had allowed him to see her mother in her, not having the courage to stand and be *Maria*. And in the same way, she had sought only the idealised relationship she had dreamed of, not the father she *did* have. But it didn't have to continue on that way, and it didn't mean that there couldn't be a relationship there. He might never have really been able to say it or show it, but deep down, despite his faults, she knew that he did love her. And for the first time in what felt like for ever, she had met with her father not beneath the blanket of pain at what he wasn't capable of, or who she was not, but with the comfort of hope as to what he might be and who she was. And no matter how much devastation her argument with Matthieu had wrought that night, if this was the one good thing she could take away from it—she would take it.

She stepped out of the small rental car feeling both emotionally exposed from her visit, but also oddly stronger and more resilient, and walked towards the front door of the beautiful property she had found nearly a month ago. Using the money that Seb had set aside for her—the account she'd once sworn never to touch—she had fallen in love with it almost the moment she had seen it and leased it for at least one year. Settled in between sunflower fields and tobacco fields, the one-storey structure was everything Matthieu's estate beside Lake Lucerne was not. Warm terracotta tiles sloped over the gentle roof topping ancient stone walls. Beautiful shutters held off the penetrating sun when it became too much and in the afternoon, as the sun passed overhead, a stunning pergola almost buckling under the weight of sprawling tendrils of clematis and honeysuckle provided shade for an outdoor courtyard that she had taken up almost daily residence in.

The villa was just under two hours from Sebastian, three from her father, and what felt like a lifetime away from Matthieu. She had thought at first that she would fall into a pattern of numb, exhausted moping—but she didn't have the luxury to do that. Not to herself, not to her child. Instead of being drained by her separation from Matthieu, from the hurtful accusations they had thrown at each other that night, she had somehow been ignited by them, driven and determined in a way she had never encountered before. Driven, beyond all else, to discover who she truly was.

She had sat down with her accounts, with her wants and needs for both herself and her child, and made plans. And while it hurt that those plans were made in Matthieu's absence, they formed a future that was created, not from fantasies and falsities, but the conversations they had once shared through nights where neither had been able to sleep. It was a future that honoured the desires of both parents.

But in the plans she was beginning to make for her own future, how she hoped to juggle parenthood with her jewellery making, for once not seeing the finances from Matthieu as a tie, but a gift that would allow her to explore both sides of who she was and what and how she wanted to be, she had found that inner sense of self, that sense of accomplishment she had felt had been missing.

For the first time in what felt like for ever, her future had a shape, had a solid direction that she had created for herself. And in that, she began to know herself. Her recent appointment with her new doctor had gone well, both her and her child flourishing here. She had even started to look at schools—which was a way off—and had bought a crib for her child. Yes, she had once imagined doing that with Matthieu and the thought of putting it up herself without his involvement did hurt, but she would do it.

As for her thoughts of Matthieu, she didn't seem able to touch them. To access them. They were sealed beneath the same closed door that she had accused him of shutting over his memories of the past. But now, she understood. Understood just a little of what and why he had been forced to do that. In time, she hoped that she'd have the courage to deal with them, as she had encouraged him to deal with his hurts. But this kindness she gave herself, because that door she had slammed shut was locked with a hope she barely dared acknowledge. Hope that he would come for her.

She had just poured herself a cup of lemon and ginger tea when the sound of a vehicle on the gravel driveway drew her attention back to the present with a little jolt of excitement. That would be the crib. She had spent far too much money on it, but for the first time she didn't mind. Money didn't have strings, or checks or balances that tied to a heart. Her brother had set her up with the fund out of love, not obligation, and she would embrace it for both herself and her child.

She put down the cup and made her way to the front doors of the villa, too busy pinning them back against the wall to see the form of the man standing in the middle of the entrance, blocking out all the light as if it was his right.

'If you could just—'

Her words caught in her throat as she took in the sight

of Matthieu, her quick, hungry eyes almost tripping over the features she'd gone to sleep imagining every night since she'd left Switzerland. The dark furrow of his brow, the strong jaw line, the impossible breadth of his shoulders and arms. All of it. She wanted it all.

Her gaze flew back to his eyes, shining a heady combination of hope, sadness and something she dared not put name to.

Matthieu felt the breath whoosh from his lungs with a sense of peace the moment his eyes finally rested on his wife. He knew, as sure as he knew anything, that he still had a mountain to climb, but allowed himself this one moment, because in all the days, nights and weeks since he had last seen her, he'd known only that a vital piece of him was missing. Something integral to his existence.

'May I come in?' he asked, promising that if she said no, he'd respect it. But also knowing that he'd come back every single day until she did let him in. Because he knew that he had hurt her. He knew that he didn't even deserve a second chance, but he desperately hoped for one.

She looked at him for the longest time and just when he thought she was about to refuse him, she frowned.

'What happened to your mouth?' she asked, shocked.

He put his thumb to the corner of his mouth where Seb had caught him and smiled ruefully. 'Nothing I didn't deserve.'

'My *brother* did that to you?' she demanded furiously

before disappearing into the dark hallway of the villa, muttering curses and dire promises of punishment.

'Maria?' he asked as he rounded the corner to find her stabbing at her phone in fury.

'Hold on.'

He frowned in confusion. This wasn't exactly how he'd planned this to be.

'Maria…'

Her name on his lips felt like a balm and if she gave him the chance, he'd say it a million times a day.

'What?' she said, as he stalked over and gently prised the phone from her hands.

'I don't want to talk about Sebastian or anything else right now. I came here to…'

She cocked her head to one side, looking, for just a moment, the way she had that first night in Iondorra. But somehow even more. She just looked and felt so much more he wasn't sure that he wouldn't explode from it. But she was still distracted by the phone, by Seb, clearly searching for anything that would buy her time, or postpone it, he couldn't tell. This wasn't what he'd wanted at all. He turned and stalked back down the corridor.

'Where are you—?' her voice came from behind him.

He bent to unhook the front shutters from where she had pinned them back and pulled one closed, before stepping out into the sunshine.

'We're starting this again. Because it's important. I'm going to get this right,' he said determinedly, pulling the second shutter too and taking a deep breath. He waited, took another. Composed himself and knocked on the door again.

When she pulled open the shutters there was an odd look on her face, part humour, part sadness and a large part confusion.

'May I come in, Maria?'

This time she seemed to take the time to consider it. And in that moment, his heart nearly stopped in his chest. Because in the long shadows pouring from either side of the hallway, he could see how much bigger their baby had become. And everything in him wanted to drop to his feet, place his hands and head on her bump and beg and plead for her forgiveness.

She moved aside before he had the chance to actually do it and gestured for him to come in.

This time he followed her down the hallway, uncaring of the villa around them, and back out into the sunlight of the most glorious courtyard he'd ever seen. Huge swathes of white and purple flowers created a canopy hanging low above their heads and the sweet smell of honeysuckle rained down upon his senses. He marvelled because this was uniquely Maria. Warm, colourful, sweet…perfect. It was everything that he'd missed the moment he had thrust her from his life.

And he shook his head at the sea of thoughts crashing against his mind. He didn't know where to start— and feared that it might all come out in a jumbled mess. He had thought this through. Had tried and tested the words over in his mind on his way here. But now, with Maria standing before him…

'Pull up a pew?' she asked. It was an olive branch and it was a chance. To start over. To get things right. But that would mean ignoring everything that had happened between them. Everything that she'd helped him see about himself, all that he'd been forced to realise was wrong within himself.

'I'll stand, but thank you.' He let out a sigh, his gaze for a moment on the stunning riotous fields of sunflowers surrounding them, while he picked his words. 'Maria, I cannot ask you to forgive me for that night. Leaving you at the restaurant was unforgivable.' Finally finding the courage, he sneaked a glance back at Maria—terrified of seeing her agreement, not even thinking for a moment he would receive clemency for it. Instead, he saw patience—a patience he did not deserve, but would take with open arms. 'You were right. About everything. I had not told you about the nightmares, or the fire, because, in truth, I didn't want you to help me see through them. Because that would have meant that I would have had to face the fact that…the fact that you had become so precious to me that I could lose you and, having lost my family, knowing the very real pain of that, I honestly didn't think that I would survive losing you or our child. And instead, I pushed you away, and lost you, all the while promising myself it would hurt less now, rather than more later.

'And it was my fear of that, the genuine terror of just how much you mean to me, just how much I have come to love you, that made me cruel. On your birthday, I took your love for me and turned it against you and that is unforgivable. So no matter what happens after today, I want you to know that no amount of time apart will change the way I feel about you. If you choose never to see me again, that is absolutely your decision. But I will always love you. You brought light to a life I didn't realise was dark. You brought truth to my soul when I didn't realise it was shrouded in secrets and guilt. And love to my empty heart. I love that I can now accept and embrace and that…that will go to you and our child always.

'The pain of the past is still there, but it is somehow…less. Honouring that pain, remembering it hasn't taken away what happened, but bringing it into the light has allowed both the hurt and the joy, the love to become a part of me, not separate or isolated, but present, and it has made me realise how much more I am with love in my life.'

This time, when he looked at his wife, he could see tears in her eyes, the slow roll down her cheek, that made him reach up and brush one away.

Maria's gaze snagged on the glint of silver that had caught her eye when he reached for her cheek. He was wearing the bracelet that had meant so much to her when she had made it. And when her gaze turned from that to her husband, all she could see was the man she loved staring back at her, glorious and proud, exulting in his feelings, and it was a marvel.

'When you first gave me this,' he said, 'all I could see was the past, was the pain, the guilt and shame that this represented to me. But, talking to Malcolm, remembering that night myself, allowing myself to re-member more… You've given me back a part of me I thought long since gone and I am awed by it, by the incredible generosity of such a thing, and the beauty of what you brought me. And now I can have this with me every single day, wherever I go.

'I can see now, that it not only represented my con-nection to the past, with my parents, and my future with you and our child, but more than that, it represents how the present could come from a past once thought damaged and burned by pain and loss, and be not only strong, and beautiful now, but hopeful and wondrous in the future.'

Tears fell freely from her eyes now. She was over-whelmed by his understanding of what she had tried to imbue into the gift, the sense of connection between them somehow even more powerful now. But she knew that she needed to speak, needed to say the words cry-ing in her heart. She covered her hands with his.

'I want… I need you to know that I heard you too.' He tried to shake off her words, as if the memory of that night was hurtful and shameful. 'No, don't. I know that our words were angry and dark, but just as you found goodness because of them, I did too. I realised that much of what you were saying was right. I was so afraid of being rejected, of being unloved myself, that instead I wove fantasies around relationships, casting myself in roles that I could shake off, move on from if those relationships failed. And it wasn't fair, to any-one, my father, brother, you or myself. I went to see my

father,' she confessed, with a small smile. 'And, no…
he's not going to suddenly change, but reframing our
relationship, not with what I *wanted* it to be, but how
it *was* and could be…it was healing, and generous, and
kind and hopefully one day loving. And I wouldn't
have had that without you or what you said that night.

'But more than that, because of that night, I forced
myself to truly take a look at who I am, who I want
to be. I'm beginning to learn about "just Maria" and,'
she said with a much larger smile, 'I like her.' Then
she frowned. '*Me*. I like me. I like discovering who I
am and, more than anything, I truly want you to come
on that journey of discovery with me. I am so thankful for that night in Iondorra. I honestly believe I fell
in love with you that first night, when in some ways
we were each more ourselves than we have been since
then. And I would very much like to spend the rest of
my life being that way with you and our child.'

'Can you say that again?' he demanded on a shaky
exhale.

'The whole thing?' Maria demanded, a little worried that she'd not be able to do it.

'No, just the most important bit.'

She smiled, instantly understanding what he was
looking for.

'I love you, Matthieu Montcour.'

'I will never tire of hearing that, Maria. And I will
never tire of saying it myself. I love you so, so much.'

Her hand reached out to caress his jaw, to reach for
him and pull him to her in a kiss that was just as much

joy and love and acceptance as it was passion and desire and need. Her heart soared as he swept her up from where she was sitting and into his arms, entwined beneath the clematis and honeysuckle as if they were weaving themselves together for ever.

Matthieu would wear the bracelet every single day for the rest of his life, through the birth of their first child—a beautiful baby girl, boisterous and full of laughter and as naughty as she could get away with— and their second, a gorgeous baby boy, sometimes serious, but always loving and considered and kind. He would wear it when he renewed his vows with his wife in the wedding he wanted to finally give her, surrounded by family and friends full of laughter, love and joy. And he would wear it as they weathered the storms that came through loss or hurt, but he would always wear it with the love that filled his heart completely for his wife, their children, his parents and himself. And he would never not be thankful that his beautiful wife had opened his heart to love and shown him that he was not the beast he had spent so long thinking himself, but someone worthy of the queen of his heart.

* * * * *

#3805 THE SPANIARD'S SURPRISE LOVE-CHILD
Passion in Paradise
by Kim Lawrence

Softhearted Gwen had always dreamed of the day tycoon Rio
would discover their child. Yet the reality is astounding! Because
when the brooding Spaniard sweeps back into her life, he
demands their daughter—and her!

#3806 MY SHOCKING MONTE CARLO CONFESSION
Passion in Paradise
by Heidi Rice

He's Monaco racing royalty and I, Belle Simpson, was his
housekeeper. But that evening, Alexi's searing gaze exhilarated
me. Five years later, I finally have the chance to reveal my secret—
Alexi's a father!

#3807 A BRIDE FIT FOR A PRINCE?
Passion in Paradise
by Susan Stephens

Samia's thrilled by the longing Prince Luca awakens within her
but knows a temporary fling is their only option. A future with him
is impossible. For the shadows of her past make Samia wholly
unsuitable...don't they?

#3808 A SCANDAL MADE IN LONDON
Passion in Paradise
by Lucy King

Kate is *mortified* when billionaire Theo discovers her secret dating
profile. Yet she can't resist his tantalizing offer to introduce her to
pleasure beyond her wildest imagination! But the biggest scandal
of all is yet to happen...

**YOU CAN FIND MORE INFORMATION ON UPCOMING HARLEQUIN TITLES,
FREE EXCERPTS AND MORE AT HARLEQUIN.COM.**

HPCNMRB0320

SPECIAL EXCERPT FROM

⊕HARLEQUIN
PRESENTS

*Theo has one goal: vengeance on his runaway bride,
Helena! But Theo can't escape the past...or the intense
connection that spectacularly reignites between them. Will
this tycoon be tempted to rewrite the rules of his revenge?*

*Read on for a sneak preview of
Michelle Smart's next story for Harlequin Presents*
His Greek Wedding Night Debt

Did she realize that every time she spoke to him, she tilted toward him? Did
she realize that she fidgeted her way through every conversation? Was she
aware that her breath hitched whenever he walked past her? Was she aware
that at that very moment her hands trembled?

"The next thing I wanted to discuss is the kitchen," she said, moving
the conversation on.

"What about it?" he asked lightly.

She tugged at the sheets of paper he'd placed his backside on. "You're
sitting on my notes."

"My apologies." Sliding smoothly off the desk, he went and sat on the
chair on the other side of her desk. "Is this better?" But she didn't respond.
Her eyes were on his, wide and stark, her fidgety body suddenly frozen.
"Helena?"

She blinked at the mention of her name and quickly looked down at
her freed notes.

"Yes. The kitchen." Despite Helena's best efforts, her voice sounded
all wrong.

It had been hard enough to breathe with Theo propped on her desk
beside her—when he'd first perched himself there, she'd feared her heart
would explode out of her chest—but when he'd moved off, she'd had to
fist her hands to stop them from grabbing hold of him. Now he was sitting
opposite her and she'd caught a sudden glimpse of his golden chest beneath
the collar of his polo shirt, and in the breath of a moment her insides had
turned to mush.

It shouldn't be like this, she thought despairingly. She'd spent three
months under Theo's intoxicating spell, riding the roller coaster of her life.

He'd had the ability to make her forget everything that mattered. Under his spell she'd believed all she needed was Theo in her life to be happy. She was sure her mother had once believed the same thing before she'd sold her soul to a monster. Theo wasn't a monster like Helena's father, but his power over Helena had been just as strong.

How could she still react so strongly to him? She'd believed the sudden detonation of their relationship had killed her feelings for him, but she saw now that she'd been hiding them, hiding them so deep inside that she'd forgotten how powerful they were until one look at him in the Staffords boardroom had seen them poke their heads out from dormancy. Now the old feelings were slapping her in the face, taunting her, and it was getting harder and harder to fight them.

Eyes now determinedly fixed on the papers on her desk, she rubbed the nape of her neck, cleared her throat and tried again. "We need to discuss the kitchen's layout. Do you still want to consult a professional chef about it?"

She knew the moment she said it that she'd made a mistake.

Something sparked in his eyes. He leaned forward a little, a satisfied smile spreading over his face. "You do remember."

"Only that neither of us can cook." She quickly fixed her gaze back on her notes, aware her face was flaming with color.

"But you asked—specifically—if I still wanted to consult a chef about the kitchen… What else do you remember?"

She tucked her hair behind her ear and wrote something nonsensical on her notepad. "Have you a chef in mind to consult?"

"Answer my question."

Her hand was shaking too much to write anything else.

"Helena."

"What?" Helena intended for her one-syllable question to come out as a challenge. She might have succeeded if her voice hadn't cracked.

"Look at me," he commanded.

Heart thrashing wildly, she breathed deeply before slowly raising her face. "What?"

His voice dropped to a murmur. "What do you remember?"

Trapped in his stare, she found herself unable to lie. "Everything."

Don't miss
His Greek Wedding Night Debt
available April 2020 wherever
Harlequin Presents books and ebooks are sold.

Harlequin.com

HPEXP0320